BREAKING THE SIEGE

Bernard O. Appiah, PhD

Copyright © 2015 Bernard O. Appiah

ISBN: 978-9988-2-2153-9

For enquiries contact the author:
Email: otopah01@yahoo.co.uk
Tel: 00 44 7572 612 947

Printed in the UK.

Lightning Source (UK) Ltd

Chapter House

Pitfield

Kiln Farm

Milton Keynes,

Buckinghamshire

MK11 3LW,
United Kingdom

Ingram Content Group

1 Ingram Blvd

La Vergne, TN 37086

United States

Lightning Source Australia PTY Ltd.

1246 Heil Quaker Blvd

Unit A1/A3 7Janine Street VIC 3179
Australia

Design: *Print Innovation (printinnovationghana@gmail.com)*

To everyone who this book will empower to break the siege of the enemy in their lives. You are a winner!

ACKNOWLEDGEMENTS

There are people you come across in life who you connect to and feel blessed.

My sincere thanks go to Rev Africanus and Dr Patience Annan (PTFC- Southampton); Rev Isaac and Mrs Stella Annan (PTFC – Southampton), thanks for being great friends. My family and I really appreciate your friendship.

In life there are those you come across who take it upon themselves to watch your back.

I appreciate Pastor Emmanuel & Prophetess Asare; and Mama Bamfo for all your love and commitment to us.

My brother and fellow labourer in the Lord's vineyard, Rev Nana Danquah (ICGC - Rhode Island) I love you.

Daniel Annan - Print Innovation Ghana, thanks for your patience and the good work done.

INTRODUCTION

There are many things that the Christian life can be likened to. These similes and metaphors grow out of the distinctive perspectives we hold of Christianity. These perspectives are developed as a result of our individual understanding of scripture, our personal experiences with God, and distinct encounters with both human and spirit entities in our universe. Like the popular ancient story of the visually impaired men of Hindustan, each of the visually impaired men's description of an elephant was based upon the part of the elephant they touched. Their personal experience with the elephant had an impact on their perspective. In as much, we may similarly hold perspectives of certain issues of life; we would rather want to know what the perspective of scripture is, since all things will pass away including every individual's perspective, but the Word shall abide forever.

It is my scriptural-informed perspective that the Christian life is not a playground rather it is a battlefield. It is an engagement with other spirit entities and humans. Even our engagement with other humans can sometimes be humans under the influence of demonic entities. It is a possibility that demon spirits speak through people, instigate certain actions of people, which are capable of creating problems for us which; we consider as human problems. This does not take away human responsibility in the circumstances and situations that confront us, but it gives us another perspective to some of the situations and things that happen around us. We need to take cognisance of the fact that there is a battle going on between the Kingdom of Satan and of the Kingdom of God. This battle is with disembodies spirits (Ephesians 6:12). And although Ephesians 6 describes it using the analogy of the Roman soldier's armour, I think it is a different kind of battle, which may not necessarily be fought literally as described in the passages. I would rather agree that the Apostle Paul uses that sort of imagery which his immediate audiences were familiar with to describe a very crucial issue throughout the life of those who have decided to accept Christ as

Lord and saviour and are therefore born into the Kingdom of God as citizens. The reason we know that this battle is real and yet the imagery chosen by Paul may not be the only way to see the battle is because in Job 1:5-8, the biblical narrative paints a picture of God and Satan having a chat, although the essence of that chat was not a friendly and indulging one, it also gives you another perspective of this battle. The content of the conversation confirms one thing, that the mission of the Satan is to steal, to kill and destroy (John). It also throws more light on the scripture in Revelations 12: 10, about Satan being the accuser of the brethren hurled down among them. This scripture portrays Satan as a prosecutor who stands before God and brings charges against God's elect. This is a battle of getting God's elect condemned in the eyes of God to shift them out of the redemptive hand of God. In this battle of control of people's lives similarly, the scriptures also portray Jesus Christ as the defence attorney – intercessor, who makes interventions for God's elect in their trial before Jehovah God (Hebrews 7:25). This is a battle of a different kind from other narratives of the scriptures earlier described.

It is as though, the closer we follow the Lord Jesus Christ, the more we advance to the front line of the conflict. This is the sobering reality that confronts every believer. No Christian can afford to be ignorant of the threatening schemes of spiritual combat, not when so dangerous an enemy is seeking the destruction of our faith, focus on God, dreams, aspirations, homes, children, investments and so on. It is critical that we are well informed regarding Satan, who prowls about as a roaring lion seeking someone to devour.

There are three formidable foes with which we contend—the world, the flesh, and the devil. The world refers to the evil system around us that is opposed to God. The flesh is our old nature that is, likewise, opposed to God and can do nothing to please Him. The devil is a fallen angel who presides over the kingdom of darkness.

Satan's strategy is to use the world and the flesh to throw our Christian lives into devastation. The moment a person is converted to Christ; he begins to meet opposition from the devil in his Christian life. His faith is constantly under attack. No believer is exempt from this warfare. Every disciple of Christ is thrown into this arena of conflict.

In ancient times, cities protected themselves from enemies by building a strong, surrounding outer wall. Even so, within the city, there would be a fortified place, which people could run to if the outer walls were breached. These inner fortresses were called 'strongholds'. In a time of war, those who sought to take the city would not only need to break through the outer wall, but take the strongholds too. This was one of the strategies adopted by the enemy in warfare.

Here are three key principles we need to take hold of:

Firstly, Satan is real. He is present from the first (Genesis 3:1) to final (Revelation 2:10) pages of scripture. The fact that there is an enemy makes spiritual struggles both possible and probable.

Second, as Christians, we are part of a spiritual battle '... *against evil rulers and authorities of the unseen world...*' (Ephesians 6:12). The enemy does not want you to get closer to God and therefore, the purpose and the potential of a spiritual you back from breaking the siege to get to the promised place.

Finally, you have been given authority '...*over all the powers of the enemy.*' (Luke 10:19). This reminds us that we have a responsibility to work with God to see demonic sieges broken for the freedom of the nations, our families and ourselves. While spiritual powers wrestle against us (Ephesians 6:12), there should be no fear within us (1 John 4:18). The Bible commands us to 'be strong and courageous' (Joshua 1:9) and commends the fight (1 Timothy 6:12).

In this book, the focus is on the siege as a warfare strategy employed by the enemy to destroy us. Through this book, you will understand what a siege is all about, how you would know you are under siege and how to break any form of siege in your life.

The content of this book is meant to remind the church of the strategy often used by the enemy against God's elect aside the other strategies from the Ephesians 6, which is sometimes over-emphasised at the expense of the other strategies and the lives of believers who remain ignorant of this effective strategy used against them. It is my desire to help Christians to be equipped and to think and fight biblically in a practical way in order to get results.

What would our churches and families look like

if we took the spiritual fight seriously, looking out for all the different and possible means of attacks? What would our marriages look like if we remembered that our battle is not against flesh and blood? What would our evangelism look like if we were wide-awake to the battle that rages? It is my prayer that the Holy Spirit will use this book to encourage and equip all to be strong in the Lord and the power of His might, to push back the enemy to advance the Kingdom of our God and His Christ.

CONTENTS

CHAPTER ONE

THE SIEGE AS A WARFARE STRATEGY

There are so many things that happen to our lives that sometimes we do not even think of how they happen and notwithstanding how to deal with them. Have you ever seen a demon before? It is not a common sight to see demons, because demons are spirits and the same way, you have not met God in person because God is a spirit. Although these spirit entities are meant to inhabit the spirit realm, they have the capabilities to influence the realm in which humans inhabit. It is therefore very important that we understand how these spirits operate so that we can deal with them appropriately. The spirit realm is not far removed from the earth realm because we understand through the scriptures that the realm of the seen came out of the invisible spirit realm and can be controlled by the invisible spirit realm (Hebrews 11:3).

The fact that the Satan and his henchmen were cast down from heaven to the earth presents us with a challenge where we have to deal with the interference of these demonic beings in our affairs in our realm (Rev 12:10). It is a challenge that the heavens threw to us at the time of relocating to the earth, Satan and his fallen angelic followers in the rebellion against God. That act has, in some sense given Satan some measure of authority over the realm occupied by humans. The scriptures refer to him as the god of this world (2 Cor. 4:4), presupposing that Satan has some measure of rulership over this realm, although originally, it has been given to man to dress it and keep it.

As a result, anyone who intends to honour Jehovah God in any way seems to run into conflict with the agenda of Satan and is bound to face his wrath. Aside Satan's reaction to individual acts and lives that honour God, he's got his own proactive plan to frustrate and where possible to destroy anything that exalts Jehovah. It is in that sense that he devises evil and strategies to carry out his purposes. The evil devises and strategies of Satan against us and our resistance to these devise and our own resolve to keep Satan defeated as God's foe is what is referred to in many circles as spiritual warfare.

Spiritual warfare is not solely like a wrestling match like some of us have come to exclusively accept in isolation to other scriptures that provides us with insight into this warfare with Satan and his cohorts. Ephesians 6 which say, *"For we do not wrestle against flesh and blood, but against principalities, against powers, against the rulers of the darkness of this age, against spiritual hosts of wickedness in the heavenly places"*. That popular WWE superstar Daniel Bryan may find it very difficult to make a return to the ring anytime soon due to neck and elbow injuries, which require a number of surgeries.

In a wrestling match, you have an opponent with whom it be assumed that sometimes; you can be down, other times he can also be down on the canvas until one is adjudged the winner after the contest. In this case, you need to be trained or have the courage and strength like John Cena or Amalinze. A Foremost of us when we hear of spiritual warfare, the only thing that comes to mind is wrestling with Spiritual Beings. It is not like exchanging of blows with the devil. When you watch World Wrestling Entertainment, you could realise that it is no child's play. Though it is true that in professional wrestling, wrestlers often assault their opponents, for which consequences can sometimes be fatal. This makes it one of the most dangerous disciplines around the world

However, there is a warfare, which does not involve the exchange of blows as in wrestling; it is a strategy adopted by the enemy against God's people that makes things to fall apart in people's lives. It is capable of creating a situation, when you have done all the things that must be done yet there is no corresponding fruitful outcome. This kind of warfare is besiegement. It has to be noted that demonic spirit forces can besiege individuals, communities, churches, cities and even nations. Let us take a look at the biblical narrative of a besiegement from the book of 2 Kings 6:24-33; 7:1-20.

"24 Sometime later, Ben-Hadad king of Aram mobilized his entire army and marched up and laid siege to Samaria. 25 There was a great famine in the city; the siege lasted so long that a donkey's

head sold for eighty shekels of silver, and a quarter of a cab of seed pods for five shekels.

26 As the king of Israel was passing by on the wall, a woman cried to him, "Help me, my lord the king!"

27 The king replied, "If the Lord does not help you, where can I get help for you? From the threshing floor? From the winepress?" 28 Then he asked her, "What's the matter?"

She answered, "This woman said to me, 'Give up your son so we may eat him today, and tomorrow we'll eat my son.' 29 So we cooked my son and ate him. The next day I said to her, 'Give up your son so we may eat him,' but she had hidden him."

30 When the king heard the woman's words, he tore his robes. As he went along the wall, the people looked, and they saw that, under his robes, he had sackcloth on his body. 31 He said, "May God deal with me, be it ever so severely, if the head of Elisha son of Shaphat remains on his shoulders today!"

32 Now Elisha was sitting in his house, and the elders were sitting with him. The king sent a messenger ahead, but before he arrived, Elisha

said to the elders, "Don't you see how this murderer is sending someone to cut off my head? Look, when the messenger comes, shut the door and hold it shut against him. Is not the sound of his master's footsteps behind him?" 33 While he was still talking to them, the messenger came down to him.

The king said, "This disaster is from the Lord. Why should I wait for the Lordany longer?"

"Elisha replied, "Hear the word of the Lord. This is what the Lord says: About this time tomorrow, a seah of the finest flour will sell for a shekel and two seahs of barley for a shekel at the gate of Samaria."

2 The officer on whose arm the king was leaning said to the man of God, "Look, even if the Lord should open the floodgates of the heavens, could this happen?"

"You will see it with your own eyes," answered Elisha, "but you will not eatany of it!"

3 Now there were four men with leprosy at the entrance of the city gate. They said to each other, "Why stay here until we die? 4 If we say, 'We'll go into the city'—the famine is there, and we will die. And if we stay here, we will die. So let's go

over to the camp of the Arameans and surrender. If they spare us, we live; if they kill us, then we die."

⁵ At dusk they got up and went to the camp of the Arameans. When they reached the edge of the camp, no one was there, ⁶ for the Lord had caused the Arameans to hear the sound of chariots and horses and a great army, so that they said to one another, "Look, the king of Israel has hired the Hittite and Egyptian kings to attack us!" ⁷ So they got up and fled in the dusk and abandoned their tents and their horses and donkeys. They left the camp as it was and ran for their lives.

⁸ The men who had leprosy reached the edge of the camp, entered one of the tents and ate and drank. Then they took silver, GOLD and clothes, and went off and hid them. They returned and entered another tent and took some things from it and hid them also.

⁹ Then they said to each other, "What we're doing is not right. This is a day of good news and we are keeping it to ourselves. If we wait until daylight, punishment will overtake us. Let's go at once and report this to the royal palace."

¹⁰ So they went and called out to the city

gatekeepers and told them, "We went into the Aramean camp and no one was there—not a sound of anyone—only tethered horses and donkeys, and the tents left just as they were."[11] The gatekeepers shouted the news, and it was reported within the palace.

[12] The king got up in the night and said to his officers, "I will tell you what the Arameans have done to us. They know we are starving; so they have left the camp to hide in the countryside, thinking, 'They will surely come out, and then we will take them alive and get into the city.'"

[13] One of his officers answered, "Have some men take five of the horses that are left in the city. Their plight will be like that of all the Israelites left here—yes, they will only be like all these Israelites who are doomed. So let us send them to find out what happened."

[14] So they selected two chariots with their horses, and the king sent them after the Aramean army. He commanded the drivers, "Go and find out what has happened." [15] They followed them as far as the Jordan, and they found the whole road strewn with the clothing and equipment the Arameans had thrown away in their headlong flight. So the

messengers returned and reported to the king. [16] Then the people went out and plundered the camp of the Arameans. So a seah of the finest flour sold for a shekel, and two seahs of barley sold for a shekel, as the Lord had said.

[17] Now the king had put the officer on whose arm he leaned in charge of the gate, and the people trampled him in the gateway, and he died, just as the man of God had foretold when the king came down to his house. [18] It happened as the man of God had said to the king: "About this time tomorrow, a seah of the finest flour will sell for a shekel and two seahs of barley for a shekel at the gate of Samaria."

[19] The officer had said to the man of God, "Look, even if the Lord should open the floodgates of the heavens, could this happen?" The man of God had replied, "You will see it with your own eyes, but you will not eat any of it!"[20] And that is exactly what happened to him, for the people trampled him in the gateway, and he died."
(2 Kings 6:24, 7:1-20).

What then is a siege?

A siege is a military blockade of a city or a fortress with the intent of conquering by attrition or assault. The term derives from *sedere*, Latin for "to sit." Siege warfare is a form of constant, low-intensity conflict characterized by one party holding a strong, static defensive position. Consequently, an opportunity for negotiation between combatants is not uncommon, as proximity and fluctuating advantage can encourage diplomacy.

The Concise Oxford Dictionary defines a siege as a military operation in which enemy forces surround a town or building, cutting off essential supplies, with the aim of compelling the surrender of those inside.

A siege is similar to the operation by a police team to compel the surrender of an armed person. When the enemy surrounds you or takes up a stand against you, preventing you from moving forward or experiencing the blessings that are truly yours, it is called a siege. A siege occurs when an attacker encounters a city or fortress that cannot be easily taken by a *coup de main* and refuses to surrender. Sieges involve surrounding the target and blocking the reinforcement or escape of troops or provision of supplies, typically coupled with attempts to reduce the fortifications by means of siege engines, artillery bombardment, mining (also known as sapping), or the use of deception or treachery to bypass defences.

Failing a military outcome, sieges can often be decided by starvation, thirst, or disease, which can afflict either the attacker or defender.

This form of siege, though, can take many months or even years, depending on the size of the stores of food the fortified position holds. During the process of circumvallated, the attacking force can be set upon by another force of enemies due to the lengthy amount of time required to starve a position. A defensive ring of forts outside the ring of circumvallated forts, called contravallation, is also sometimes used to defend the attackers from outside enemy forces.

A siege is normally adopted as a warfare strategy when a nation realises or an army realises that their target is too strong for them to go combat in terms of foot by foot or may be in terms of face to face combat then they have to use the siege as a method of conquering their enemies. It is worth noting that this form of warfare strategy is dynamic depending upon the strength of the enemy. There have been instances where some powerful nations besiege other nations through the imposition of certain sanctions such as offensive arms embargo, freezing of assets and access to funds, economic sanctions, creating no-fly zones and even using neighbouring border countries as stations to create hardship and panic among the populace of the country under attack. The combinations of these sanctions are meant to weaken the military capability of the enemy to conquer them.

For clarity of the above paragraph, you need to understand that in military warfare or in warfare strategy in modern times, sometimes, certain countries can or another nation can besiege another country without necessarily going to the country to touch the inhabitants of that country, and it is as effective as bombing the people and killing them. When an army surrounds a city to make sure that nothing goes into the city, and nothing comes out of the city; their food supplies and everything run out, and they famish and die out of hunger. They are in a siege state or condition.

Although they may not bomb them physically and there are no sending of bows and arrows and ammunitions to the city, yet they are dying within because they have been surrounded. They die on their own accord, why? Because you have blocked certain vital supplies from them that they can no longer live a normal life without them. This is the state most of us believers are; we are stacked are not able to access the blessing that are promised in the bible.

As already mentioned, the enemy against individuals can effectively apply this strategy of besiegement. It is by the application of this strategy that to lay siege against an individual would be to surround someone's life with methods, which may include seduction techniques (honey traps), messages of terror and fear, negative re-orientation and conditioning until he or she agrees to the new terms of authority and control that his opponent wants to introduce in his life. Samson was besieged by the Philistine when they used Delilah as the agent to weaken him for them to be able to take control of him.

He was having a wall of defence by God (a gift of strength). Samson handed over the keys to the wall of defence to Delilah, making it possible for the Philistines to have access to Samson and take him captive.

"... Samson lay until midnight, and arose at midnight, and laid hold of the doors of the gate of the city, and the two posts, and plucked them up, bar and all, and put them on his shoulders, and carried them up to the top of the mountain that is before Hebron. It came to pass afterward, that he loved a woman in the valley of Sorek, whose name was Delilah. ⁵ The lords of the Philistines came up to her, and said to her, "Entice him, and see in which his great strength lies, and by what means we may prevail against him, that we may bind him to afflict him; and we will each give you eleven hundred pieces of silver."

⁶ Delilah said to Samson, "Please tell me where your great strength lies, and what you might be bound to afflict you."

⁷ Samson said to her, "If they bind me with seven green cords that were never dried, then shall I become weak, and be as another man."

⁸ Then the lords of the Philistines brought up to her seven green cords which had not been dried, and she bound him with them. ⁹ Now she had an ambush waiting in the inner room. She said to him, "The Philistines are on you, Samson!" He broke the cords, as a string of tow is broken when it touches the fire. So his strength was not known.

10 Delilah said to Samson, "Behold, you have mocked me, and told me lies: now please tell me with which you might be bound."... Delilah said to Samson, "Until now, you have mocked me and told me lies. Tell me with what you might be bound."

He said to her, "If you weave the seven locks of my head with the web."

14 She fastened it with the pin, and said to him, "The Philistines are on you, Samson!" He awakened out of his sleep, and plucked away the pin of the beam, and the web....18 When Delilah saw that he had told her all his heart, she sent and called for the lords of the Philistines, saying, "Come up this once, for he has told me all his heart." Then the lords of the Philistines came up to her, and brought the money in their hand. 19 She made him sleep on her knees; and she called for a man, and shaved off the seven locks of his head; and she began to afflict him, and his strength went from him. 20 She said, "The Philistines are upon you, Samson!"

He awoke out of his sleep, and said, "I will go out as at other times, and shake myself free." But he didn't know that Yahweh had departed from him.²¹ The Philistines laid hold on him, and put out his eyes; and they brought him down to Gaza, and bound him with fetters of brass; and he ground at the mill in the prison. ²² However the hair of his head began to grow again after he was shaved.

²³ The lords of the Philistines gathered them together to offer a great sacrifice to Dagon their god, and to rejoice; for they said, "Our god has delivered Samson our enemy into our hand." ²⁴ When the people saw him, they praised their god; for they said, "Our god has delivered our enemy and the destroyer of our country, who has slain many of us, into our hand." (Judges 16:1-24)

The stronghold of Samson was taken over by his enemies through Delilah. And this may be just one way the enemy employed as the tactics of besiegement against Samson. The enemy's besiegement of your life may not be the exact same way, but it is for you to recognise that an enemy can besiege and therefore, one has to be on their guard all the time, on the lookout for any works of besiegement.

In applying this warfare tactic, it is therefore, worthwhile to note that to besiege a city; armed force surrounds and isolates it, while usually continuing its attacks upon it. In general, siege warfare involves bombardment (anything from, in ancient times, arrows or flaming arrows, catapulted rocks, or even catapulted corpses of plague victims to cause epidemics among the defenders, also in more contemporary times, artillery and "smart bombs") and cut-off of supply, which causes starvation and deprivation. It was usually only after the city surrendered, or was greatly weakened, that infantry entered. There have been many great sieges of cities throughout human history.

The biblical narrative reveals this warfare strategy as used in the day, when kings went to fight against their enemies, the first thing they did was to besiege the city or the people that they wanted to attack as in the case from 2 Kings 6:24-33; 7:1-20. And through the process of besieging, they stopped every food supply, spiritual nourishment, trading (product selling and buying) that was coming from the outside of that city that they were besieging. For instance, when a besiegement took place around a city, (most of the cities from those biblical days were surrounded by walls), the people in the besieged city will begin to starve, fall into despair, fear, distress, doubt, hopelessness, lack of faith, and anguish of soul, because of the besiege that is stopping the resources which sustains their lives.

Historical and Biblical examples of the siege warfare

In medieval times, there was one such occurrence during the siege of Nicea (first crusade). The crusaders cut off the heads of their enemies and threw them inside their walls, so that they may create an image of panic, alarm and fear inside the enemies' camp.

Besiegement was such an effective warfare strategy that there are records of some use sieges in the bible some of which was upon God's instruction.

1. God gave instruction to the Israelites on how they were to besiege cities:

"When you draw near to a city to fight against it, offer terms of peace to it. And if its answer to you is peace and it opens to you, then all the people who are found in it shall do forced labour for you and shall serve you. But if it makes no peace with you, but makes war against you, then you shall besiege it; and when The Lord your God gives it into your hand you shall put all its males to the sword, but the women and the little ones, the cattle, and everything else in the city, all its spoil; you shall take as booty for yourselves; and you shall enjoy the spoil of your enemies, which The Lord your God has given you.

When you besiege a city for a long time, making war against it in order to take it, you shall not destroy its trees by wielding an axe against them; for you may eat of them, but you shall not cut them down. Are the trees in the field men that they should be besieged by you? Only the trees which you know are not trees for food you may destroy and cut down that you may build siege works against the city that makes war with you, until it falls." (Deuteronomy 20:10-20)

2. Siege as a warfare strategy by some OT Biblical Leaders

Under the leadership of Joshua, during their taking of the Promised Land, the Israelites besieged a number of Canaanite cities, the most famous of which was Jericho.

"And Joshua passed on from Libnah, and all Israel with him, to Lachish, and laid siege to it, and assaulted it"

"And Joshua passed on with all Israel from Lachish to Eglon; and they laid siege to it, and assaulted it" (Joshua 10: 31, 34)

"Now Jericho was shut up from within and from without because of the people of Israel; none went out, and none came in. And The Lord said to Joshua, "See, I have given into your hand Jericho, with its king and mighty men of valour." (Joshua 6:1-2)

3. Besiegement as a punishment from God

There are also examples from scripture of God warning his people of allowing the enemy to besiege them as a form of punishment.

a. God warned the Israelites that if they became corrupt, the tables would be turned on them - God would allow their enemies to besiege them in their own cities:

"Because you did not serve The Lord your God with joyfulness and gladness of heart, by reason of the abundance of all things, therefore, you shall serve your enemies whom The Lord will send against you, in hunger and thirst, in nakedness, and in want of all things; and he will put a siege of iron upon your neck, until he has destroyed you."

The Lord will bring a nation against you from afar, from the end of the earth, as swift as the eagle flies, a nation whose language you do not understand, a nation of stern countenance, who shall not regard the person of the old or show favour to the young, and shall eat the offspring of your cattle and the fruit of your ground, until you are destroyed; who also shall not leave you grain, wine, or oil, the increase of your cattle or the young of your flock, until they have caused you to perish. They shall besiege you in all your towns, until your high and fortified walls, in which you trusted, come down throughout all your land; and they shall besiege you in all your towns throughout all your land, which The Lord your God has given you. And you shall eat the offspring of your own body, the flesh of your sons and daughters, whom The Lord your God has given you, in the siege and in the distress with which your enemies shall distress you." (Deuteronomy 28:47-53)

b. The Israelites ignored God's warning, and so they were besieged and conquered, first the northern kingdom of Israel at Samaria by the Assyrians in 721 BC, and afterwards the southern kingdom of Judah at Jerusalem by the Babylonians in 586 BC.

"Then the king of Assyria [see Ancient Empires - Assyria] invaded all the land and came to Samaria, and for three years he besieged it. In the ninth year of Hoshea the king of Assyria captured Samaria, and he carried the Israelites away to Assyria, and placed them in Halah, and on the Habor, the river of Gozan, and in the cities of the Medes."

"And this was so, because the people of Israel had sinned against The Lord their God, who had brought them up out of the land of Egypt from under the hand of Pharaoh king of Egypt, and had feared other gods and walked in the customs

of the nations whom The Lord drove out before the people of Israel, and in the customs which the kings of Israel had introduced." (2 Kings 17:5-8) *"And in the ninth year of his reign, in the tenth month, on the tenth day of the month, Nebuchadnezzar king of Babylon [see Ancient Empires - Babylon] came with all his army against Jerusalem, and laid siege to it; and they built siege works against it round about. So the city was besieged till the eleventh year of King Zedekiah.*

On the ninth day of the fourth month, the famine was so severe in the city that there was no food for the people of the land. Then a breach was made in the city; the king with all the men of war fled by night by the way of the gate between the two walls, by the king's garden, though the Chaldeans were around the city. And they went in the direction of the Arabah. But the army of the Chaldeans pursued the king, and overtook him in the plains of Jericho; and all his army was scattered from him. Then they captured the king, and brought him up to the king of Babylon at Riblah, who passed sentence upon him. They slew the sons of Zedekiah before his eyes, and put out the eyes of Zedekiah, and bound him in fetters, and took him to Babylon.

In the fifth month, on the seventh day of the month - which was the nineteenth year of King Nebuchadnezzar, king of Babylon - Nebuzaradan, the captain of the bodyguard, a servant of the king of Babylon, came to Jerusalem. And he burned the house of The Lord [see Why Babylon?, Temples and Raiders Of The Lost Ark], and the king's house and all the houses of Jerusalem; every great house he burned down. And all the army of the Chaldeans, who were with the captain of the guard, broke down the walls around Jerusalem."
(2 Kings 25:1-10)

c. At the time of Sennacherib king of Assyria, against Hezekiah, the siege was raised by a Divine interposition, as foretold by Isaiah the prophet.

"10 At that time the servants of Nebuchadnezzar king of Babylon came up to Jerusalem, and the city was besieged. 11 Nebuchadnezzar king of Babylon came to the city while his servants were besieging it, 12 and Jehoiachin the king of Judah went out to the king of Babylon, he, and his mother, and his servants, and his princes, and his officers; and the king of Babylon CAPTURED HIM in the eighth year of his reign. 13 He carried out from there all the treasures of Yahweh's

house, and the treasures of the king's house, and cut in pieces all the vessels of GOLD, which Solomon king of Israel had made in Yahweh's temple, as Yahweh had said. ¹⁴ He carried away all Jerusalem, and all the princes, and all the mighty men of valor, even ten thousand captives, and all the craftsmen and the smiths. No one remained, except the poorest people of the land. ¹⁵ He carried away Jehoiachin to Babylon, with the king's mother, the king's wives, his officers, and the chief men of the land. He carried them into captivity from Jerusalem to Babylon.¹⁶ All the men of might, even seven thousand, and the craftsmen and the smiths one thousand, all of them strong and fit for war, even them the king of Babylon brought captive to Babylon."
(2Kings 24:10-16)

A siege in all the above cases talks about being surrounded by physical places or groups or persons in order to prevent the people inside from receiving food or water or something of value. It is the action of surrounding a fortified place and isolating it while continuing to attack. Even though a siege is a military word or is mostly used in the warfare arena, it has a spiritual parallel for Christians because we wrestle not against flesh and blood but against powers of darkness and principalities.

In siege warfare, one army surrounds a fortified area with the intent to capture it. In the same way, the devil besiege a believer when believer's life begins to experience a denial from the good promises or supplies that are to come from God, which is a result of blockades, impediments and spiritual sanctions imposed on him or her from the devil.

Satan's first tactic is to surround us and cut off our supplies. It is his desire to get us out of the Word, out of fellowship, out of prayer, out of progress, etc. Just as the ancient army sought to cut off their enemy from food, water, and contact with allies who could aid them, likewise, Satan seeks to cut off the believer from the life-giving Word of God- the Bible, from fellowship of other believers, and from prayer. If you find yourself drifting away from firm contact with other Christians - watch out! If your devotion to prayer is waning, and your consistent study of the Word is lacking - be careful! You are in the first stages of being besieged.

However, the devil usually cannot touch you without your cooperation. The devil cannot destroy you except there is a way by which he can use. Satan afflicted Job only because God gave the permission to do so. As a believer, you are fortified or have a protection around you. The bible says God **surrounds** His people like a mountain that surrounds Jerusalem so you are automatically preserved by God so long as you live as a born-again person. Even though the devil might try to attack by besieging you, it would not work because you have a stronghold through the weapon of God in your life.

CHAPTER TWO

RELATIONSHIP BEWTEEN STRONGHOLDS AND SIEGES

A siege is normally a deliberate blockade to your portion of blessing from God or it creates boundaries between you and God. The space, which has been created or protected from an external influence, is what has been referred to as a stronghold. The stronghold that has been created can be good or bad. It can be space for the exclusive operational influence for the devil or for the Lord. This means that if it is for a good course, it prevents the enemy from invasion.

For example, the devil can build a blockade through certain difficult circumstances, such that you will not believe the word of God anytime you hear it; this is the siege of the devil which will result in you becoming rebellious to God's word; if unchallenged for a long while, it ends up being a stronghold of the devil over your life.

On the other hand, you might be a person who is determined in every situation you might find yourself by standing on God's word to rebuke the devil so that you will not be overtaken by the situation. You might have built a strong faith in God's word for your life like that of Shadrach, Meshach, and Abednego which they demonstrated when the king, Nebuchadnezzar told them to worship his image of gold. The stronghold usually has high walls and a tower to see the enemy coming from a distance in order to prepare. In Proverbs, having a stronghold is a good source of protection from the enemy.

"The name of the Lord is a strong tower; the righteous run to it and are safe." (Proverbs 18:10)

In the same Old Testament, we find that David hid from King Saul in wilderness strongholds at Horesh serving as a means of protection from an enemy.

"And David stayed in strongholds in the

wilderness, and remained in the mountains in the Wilderness of Ziph. Saul sought him every day, but God did not deliver him into his hand....Then the Ziphites came up to Saul at Gibeah, saying, "Is David not hiding with us in strongholds in the woods, in the hill of Hachilah, which is on the south of Jeshimon?"

(1 Samuel 23:14, 19)

These were physical structures usually caves, high on a mountainside, and were very difficult to attack. A stronghold is therefore a source of protection for you from the devil, as in the case of David also. A stronghold can be a source of defence for the devil's influence in your life, where demonic or sinful activity is actually defended within your walls of thought. It was this imagery in mind that the inspired writers of the Bible to adapt the word "stronghold" to define powerful vigorously protected spiritual interests.

In the New Testament, however, there is a reference to pulling down strongholds. This is because people were depending on things other than God for their comfort and security. Paul used the word *strongholds* in the New Testament to metaphorically describe the Christian's spiritual battle: Another translation is this:

"For though we walk in the flesh, we do not war after the flesh: (For the weapons of our warfare are not carnal, but mighty through God to the pulling down of strong holds)"
(2 Corinthians 10:3-4)

The bottom line is, Jesus Christ is a strong tower and a stronghold that we must learn to hide in. Anything else that we are depending on, trusting in, relying on, in the place of God, or any part of your life being kept in isolation from God's touch either by yourself or by the devil. This is a stronghold that needs to be pulled down. Since it is a good thing to have positive strongholds in our life and not a threat to our service and relationship with the Lord, our attention has been on the negative strongholds that have been created by the devil.

A failure to remove strongholds, would nullify any victory in the course of time as the forces that control the strongholds could come back charging at us. Since an invader could not occupy every square mile of land, as soon as the army moved, the enemy in the stronghold could reoccupy conquered territory. When you come to

Christ, the Lord takes up residence in your life. You become the Lord's property, his grounds where he sows seeds for our benefit and for those who are connected to us and from then on the battle for territory with Satan begins. Satan is not willing to give ground to the Lord because he does not want us to be who God wants us to be.

To do this, Satan constructs strongholds, whether physical, emotional, psychological, mental or spiritual, which feed our Adamic nature and weaknesses. One thing to remember is that without some measure of cooperation with Satan, it is almost impossible for him to destroy us or have us to move away from the presence of God. Satan works to keep as many strongholds standing in our lives as he can. His desire is to keep us blind to the Gospel of Christ, so that we die in a lost condition.

"But even if our gospel is veiled, it is veiled to those who are perishing, whose minds the god of this age has blinded, who do not believe, lest the light of the gospel of the glory of Christ, who is the image of God, should shine on them" (2 Corinthians 4:3-4).

It's imperative for us to have these satanic

strongholds pulled down. If you do not remove them, you invite failure and defeat in your spiritual walk.

Thoughts as strongholds

A stronghold can also be anything that you have placed your confidence in for comfort and security. In the Old Testament a stronghold was a fortified city usually located atop a hill making it difficult for the enemy to attack. Strongholds do not appear in our lives overnight; they are built stone upon stone over time as in a stone building. As we reinforce certain thoughts and allow them space (and time) in our minds. The longer, and more often, we think and dwell on things we ought not to, the further we strengthen these strongholds and the more powerful they become. They must be dismantled the same way they were erected – stone-by-stone.

Explaining strongholds from the negative sense, Ed Silvoso, the founder of Harvest Evangelism and International Transformation Network, describes a stronghold as a mindset impregnated with hopelessness that causes us to accept something that we know is contrary to the will of God. It is important to recognise that when we speak of strongholds of the mind, we are not talking about random thoughts but rather a pattern of thinking produced from a fortified framework of mind-set. We are talking about a wrong pattern of thinking that rules your life, attitude, character, and lifestyle that you are bound to and are having a hard time breaking loose from. In other words, stronghold is built in your thoughts and it is consolidated, over time it penetrates into your unconscious mind and becomes mindset that controls your life. It can be either positive or negative.

Thoughts are planted like seeds, and the more you think them (tend them, nurture them, water them), the more they grow. This is why we are to meditate on the Word day and night as admonished in Joshua 1:8. Then you will build strongholds of God's thoughts that will cause you success and prosperity in all your doing. You will only prosper and succeed to the degree you think like God.

In most cases of "Christians", whether physical, emotional, psychological, or spiritual in origin, strongholds are best defined as areas of exclusive control to Satan, in which the enemy has free rein to strengthen and extend his hold over the individual under his domination.

The main point is that a stronghold has an operational relationship with a siege; it serves as a source for the devil's influence in our lives. As a stronghold is an area in a person's life where the enemy has taken hold or is operating with less resistance, a siege is a blockade or barrier that the enemy has used to prevent the believer from receiving the blessing and the promises of God. As in the main text from 2 Kings 6, even though Israelites have not been in direct combat with their enemies yet they were dying, which is a sign of a siege and at the same time a stronghold because they have caused total chaos in the city of Samaria. Similarly, you can have nicely dressed individuals who are mentally damaged by the enemy through deceit, charade of lies and negative image of self; it is only a matter of time when that damage would begin to show on the outside through the individuals' self-destructive tendencies.

Public Conviction strongholds

There are certain convictions that can be held as views, positions, perceptions, thoughts, philosophy, and even ideology by group of persons or even nations, which can serve as a stronghold. If these are not held in line with the word of God, they can be subject to the prince of the power of the air, the spirit who now works in the sons of disobedience and taken as a stronghold to hold people in bondage. Sometimes, strongholds could be created by forces of evil through certain cultural practices, self-expression and philosophy of people, in order to hold them back from what God has for them.

Individual thoughts and strongholds can be pulled down, but so can ways of thinking that prevail in a group of people. Even the evil forces in the heavenlies that have gained a stronghold in certain areas or places because of the practices and thinking of the people who live there can be pulled down.

When you run to your house and lock all the doors and windows, and pushed furniture in front of them, and you get your guns, knives, and brooms and you wait. You have created a stronghold of protection from outside attack.

However, you realise that not all enemies

operate from the outside, but inside with you. People have been ensnared and held in bondage by the enemy simply because there are a lot of things that society may accept today as the normative way of life and even reasoning and have therefore become strongholds. God says, you should tear it down. We say, "But God, it's fun, and it feels good!" and "everyone accepts it", "even the celebrities and well-meaning people in society do not see anything wrong with it?" We do not have a problem being locked in these strongholds possibly because they have become the normative way of living. God wants o pull them down.

The reason strongholds are so hard to pull down in our lives is because we helped to build them up. I do understand that sometimes it's hard tearing down such things in our lives that are bad for us. This is because we have spent years investing in them. The enemy only introduces us to the stronghold but we fortify them. Satan doesn't just come upon our lives and establish strongholds without our consent.

Stronghold of Carnality

Ungodly strongholds are formed when we go against the counsel of God's word. Ephesians 4:27 says, *"Neither give place to the devil."* God has provided a stronghold for us through Jesus Christ that the enemy cannot penetrate. However, over the years, we have weakened it through sin and rebellion. So, there are holes through the walls. There are breaches in our defence.

This is why God would say in the Old Testament, I need someone to stand in the gap; I need someone to make up the hedge. Anywhere there is an opening that is a place we have given to the enemy that allows him access to our lives. We all like God's overall stronghold of protection, but we do not like closing up all the little holes in the wall.

"¹ Now the serpent was more subtle than any animal of the field which Yahweh God had made. He said to the woman, "Has God really said, 'You shall not eat of any tree of the garden?'"

² The woman said to the serpent, "We may eat fruit from the trees of the garden, ³ but not the fruit of the tree which is in the middle of the garden.

God has said, 'You shall not eat of it. You shall not touch it, lest you die.'"

⁴ The serpent said to the woman, "You won't surely die, ⁵ for God knows that in the day you eat it, your eyes will be opened, and you will be like God, knowing good and evil."

⁶ When the woman saw that the tree was good for food, and that it was a delight to the eyes, and that the tree was to be desired to make one wise, she took some of its fruit, and ate; and she gave some to her husband with her, and he ate it, too."(Genesis 3:1-6)

In Genesis 3:1-6 above, we find the very first stronghold of sin. Let's look at four elements that are present in the building of an ungodly stronghold; Seduction, lies, building, and sealing. In verse 1, we see the subtle seduction of Satan. In verse 4, we see the lie. In verse 5 we see the building upon the lie. Notice who has done all the work on the stronghold at this point, Satan. Remember, the enemy cannot build a stronghold in your life without your consent. He can only introduce it to you. This was his introduction to Eve. In verse 6, Eve's rebellion seals the stronghold, and then she shares with Adam. That is the nature of a stronghold. When you are convinced that it is good, you share it with others.

The four basic elements of a Godly stronghold are instruction, truth, building, and sealing. God gives us instruction from his Holy word. God is not a man whom He should lie so we accept His word as truth. From studying the Bible, line upon line, precept upon precept and by going through life experiences, we build upon what God has taught us. Then through submission and obedience, we seal the stronghold and reap the blessings.

Now let's talk about the kinds of strongholds that are generally formed in church.
(I Corinthians 3:10, 11).

In the church, Jesus Christ is the foundation. We are instructed to be careful of what we allow to be built on top of that foundation. Religious strongholds are often formed in the church because we sometimes accept these new things without adequately checking them out. People are then left, used, abused, and confused when these things do not work out. The pattern of development is the same as, we saw with Eve and the serpent. There is seduction, followed by lies. Then building on those lies and finally we seal the deal by giving in to it.

In the book of Ezekiel 13:4-16, God was speaking to the religious leaders. He tells them that He already has a stronghold, but sin and rebellion have left some holes in it. All God wanted was for the leaders to stand in the gaps, make up the hedges, and repair the holes through the wall. These vain religious leaders wanted to develop new strongholds. They wanted the people to rely on them and not on God. Their goal was to seduce, to lie, to build upon those lies, and get the people to buy into it. Things have not changed a lot since the time of Ezekiel. God is trying to get His people ready for the storm, but many leaders are talking about how peaceful things are going to be.

God is talking about repentance, forgiveness, and restoration and all many leaders seem to be talking about is how you can get a blessing. God is saying, fortify the old stronghold, and leaders are saying let's build a brand new one altogether. By creating new strongholds these leaders profit because we become dependent on them and their books instead of God and His book.

In verse 10, we see the entire pattern. First, the seduction, afterwards the lie about peace. Then they build up a wall. Finally, the people begin to seal the wall. Strongholds form when we buy into what men say without checking with God. Man seduces, lies, and builds, but we are the ones that seal it. From verses 11-16, we notice the phrase that is repeated, "daubed with untempered mortar". What this phrase means is that the cement that you are using to seal this new stronghold together is weak. It is not properly mixed. It may last for a season, but it will not endure. This is the same thing that God is saying about your rationale for why you are not pulling down the strongholds; it's weak. The excuses that you give God as to why you have not changed or grown up in the faith are weak. The logic and reasoning is untempered and is not holding together too well.

In the verse 14, ungodly strongholds do not last! If you do not start to pull down the strongholds in your life, God is going to cause them to fall down on you. God says He will do this so you can see the true foundation. Is Christ really your foundation?

When the rubble is cleared away what will be revealed? Was your foundation really greed, power, fame, or some other vanity?

Notice the verse 11 which says, "Say unto them which daub it". There is no mention of those that are seducing, lying and putting up the wall. God will deal with them later. These verses are talking to you. The enemy will always seduce and lie and even stack the bricks for us but that means nothing if we don't seal it!

A stronghold is more than a stack of bricks. We decide whether or not we're going to apply the mortar. We ultimately decide if it will stand or not. Why is it easier to develop ungodly strongholds than Godly ones? The reason is Satan does not mind if we use untempered mortar. He wants us to do a rush job and seal things based on emotions and not on God. Then when it falls on us, he laughs.

However, God requires that our mortar be hardened. The word tempered means mixed in satisfying proportions. So God says, do not rely on just your thoughts and emotions to make this decision. You need to mix in some prayer, some faith, some Bible study, some solid counsel and maybe even some fasting. When we get that all mixed in together in the right proportions, we will be in a position to take decisions that will not only hold but will bless us. Tempered mortar requires patience to get things mixed proportionately. Possibly I have too much emotion in this decision. Maybe I do not have enough counsel on this decision. This is how we temper the mortar to establish godly strongholds.

Tempering means to make stronger and more resilient stance through hardship. This process often involves heat. When steel or glass is tempered, it goes through the furnace. Whether you are building an ark like Noah or having the roof replaced on your home, you do not just start slapping on the adhesive.

Satan seduces, lies, and builds on lies. He depends on us to keep making half-mixed, weak decisions to seal his strongholds. God instructs you in truth. He builds upon that truth through His word. God then tempers the mortar of our souls in His refining fire so that all the impurities are burned away, and we can create a firm bond in the stronghold. When it comes to strongholds, it's not enough to just stack on bricks. Satan cannot hurt us, and God cannot help us until we seal the deal. When we seal with God, we obtain a stronghold stronger than any hold the devil may have in our life today.

Many of us attend church for one hour a week, listen to the message and go home. To make it worse, in some churches the message is only ten minutes. The rest of the week their thinking, values and views are shaped by the world, and then they wonder why they cannot get the victory in their personal lives. You cannot break those strongholds down through one sermon a week while you rebuild and reinforced the few rocks that were pulled down in the service, by the time you have finished reading the Sunday paper.

CHAPTER THREE

SYMPTOMS AND SIGNS OF BESIEGEMENT

As believers in Christ, it is important we understand how to identify the besiegement of the enemy in order to be able to combat it effectively. It is a fact that you cannot stop the enemy from attacking, but you can stop him from winning. Information such as presented throughout this chapter would equip you to be capable to recognise when the enemy is on the prowl and when he has actually built siege works against you. In some circumstances, you may not be able to stop him from building those siege works, but you can dismantle them all together when you realise it has been built. However, it is also possible to build your defences to make it difficult and even impossible for him to besiege you.

From the scriptural text and biblical narrative

we have used for the basis of this discussion, I am going to show you some of the signs that when present in your life serves as an indicator that you might have been besieged by the enemy. We have established in the previous chapter that the strategies adopted by the enemy for attack are varied. There are times his strategy of engagement is very subtle and can go unrecognised until the damage is done.

We would take a look at some of them from the scriptural text.

Stagnation and lack of progress

There was a situation in Samaria where Ben-Hadad had besieged the entire city of Samaria, the situation created panic in the city and because of that no one went out of the city. Samaria was the capital of the Northern Kingdom of ancient Israel. Similar to today's capital cities, it was a hub for governance, national treasury, storage among others and therefore, besieging it meant that there was a cut of the supply to it. According to the text, nothing entered the city or came out of the city. The city came to a complete halt and for that matter, not making any progress at all.

Similar to the experience of Samaria, whenever people are besieged, nothing goes in and nothing comes out. When life becomes stagnant to the extent that no matter how much you put in you do not get anything out, in other words, you do not reap what you had sown. You could even as an employer invested in training people and when they are at their peak of performance, they leave and join other rival companies. You put in so much into your life through hard work, like the farmer who plants a crop and hopes to harvest so much only to unexpectedly harvest so little below what is normally expected.

There are people of great potential and promise judging by their determination, hard work and willingness to sacrifice for a future gain, only for the future to arrive to have so little to show for all those years of hard work and sacrifice.

Many may succeed through the same way or step you are taking, or you may even show them the way yet they will pass or become successful, and you will fail.

You have to understand that this is one of the strategies the devil uses to besiege you, to cut you off from your supplies. Sometimes, the enemy causes you to fall out of favour with particular people who are crucial to your livelihood and by so doing cut you off from specific resources critical for your sustenance. In my life time, I have seen previously successful sports men and women decline because they parted company with their trainers; company profits have slumped and some have notwithstanding folded up when a CEO left; students have failed exams because the tutor for that particular course left the institution where they studied.

Additionally, you could find certain football players leave a particular team and the team's fortunes changes because they may lose their sponsorship with certain companies or even may fail to sell merchandise of the team to raise money to the team. In all of these cases, separation from vital resources turns out to be a major problem for their continued sustenance and success.

The enemy's plan is to besiege you to isolate you from your vital supplies, to stall your progress and to cause you to stagnate in all you do. Therefore, arise and see it and avoid it happening.

Life in itself is an organism, and organisms grow and so when organisms are disconnected from internal and external connections for their sustenance, they die. The absence of growth in your life may rightly be you have been besieged if indeed you had done all there is to make reasonable progress with your life. You may well consider stepping up your prayer to break every siege that might have been built against you.

Continuous Experiences of Famine

The result of cutting off supplies from Samaria through the besiegement created artificial famine. Accessibility to the needed resources was restricted, and therefore, resources continually became scarce until they were totally run out. Their farmlands lay in the fields where Ben-Hadad and his men were laying in wait and therefore, the resources were available and legally theirs, but they could not have access. In most cases, famine is caused when there is food shortage due to a dip in rainfall levels in the cultivating seasons and sometimes also due to lack of proper storage facilities and technology for long-term storage of surpluses over the years. As the case was in Samaria, the famine was caused due to the inaccessibility of food from the fields because the enemy had been besieged it.

When you realise that there is famine in your life, which is not caused by lack of rain – the Lord's provision, but no access to what have been provided for you, or you produce. You might be experiencing famine not as if you are a slothful man or woman. You are taking all the initiatives, when opportunities come, you try to also grab them but they do not yield their due for you. It means you are besieged.

In the book of II Kings 6:24 in which in we read, the bible says that there was a famine in Samaria not because it was not raining or the land was so bad that when they plant anything, it will not grow. It was raining, but the fact was that the enemy has taken hold of their land. The land where they were supposed to go and plant, the enemies were there and they could not go.

There might come a time in your life when you realise that you are experiencing famine, it is not because you do not have opportunities; you have the opportunities but the opportunities do not yield how much they are supposed to yield to you. You realise that not that you do not take initiative but somewhere along the line it is stifled. It is not as though you do not have creativity, but your creativity is not yielding enough. This creativity may sometimes end up in all kinds of problems. You really know what to do to make you prosperous; you know what to do to give the life you are looking for and yet when you do it nothing comes out of it.

Your life has become like what Abraham Lincoln went through at some point in his life. He failed as a businessman, when he turned to politics and was defeated in his first try for the legislature, again defeated in his initial attempt to be nominated for Congress, defeated in his application to be commissioner of the General Land Office, defeated in the senatorial election of 1854, defeated in his efforts for the vice-presidency in 1856, and defeated in the senatorial election of 1858. In all his failings, he was doing all he could to make him successful yet failure was the outcome.

When you see this sign as a believer or someone who believes the Word of God, then devil is at work because he makes you famish in a desperate moment of not getting from what you put in. You might not be physically sick or your job may not be taken away from you; you are working hard yet you do not yield much. It is a sign that you have been besieged.

Lack of Sustainability

Due to the situation as discussed above, there was no sustainability of the resources within Samaria. The siege created an acute shortage to the extent that no matter how hard they tried to manage what they had in the city it was enough to sustain them. The lack also meant that the price of food was also fluctuating, and the fluid nature of the economic situation meant that the people had to resort to unconventional food to sustain them.

When there is no sustainability to what you receive, have or experience, it is a sign that you have been besieged. When you lose what you have so easily, whether it is the anointing, favour, money or even your job it is a sign that you have been besieged. Among other credible factors for these occurrences in your life there is the need to assess your life to determine whether the enemy has besieged you and respond appropriately. It was the prevailing condition that made Elisha to prophesy that the next-day food was going to be in abundance.

You have to understand that sometimes everything in your life becomes fluid, to the extent that there is no sustainability. Sometimes, you may be up a little, the following day you are down. You are happy today the next day you are unhappy that people just get tired of you. When things like that happen to your life, you must know that you have been besieged. One of the things about God's promises is that God gives His power to make riches, and He adds no sorrow to it (Proverbs 10:22). This means that everything about your life that God gives there is no sorrow to it.

When you begin to experience sorrow with it, or what you have becomes fluid and not stable then it means that there is something wrong about it. You need to check it. Everything becomes or everything goes waste, everything sublimes, everything that you think you could gather and hold on to just go through your fingers; nothing stands.

Self-destructive Tendencies

People sustaining themselves in Samaria had become a problem and as a result have developed behaviours and appetite for things considered an abomination. The narrative describes a dire situation when a woman appealed to the king for arbitration. The matter was about an agreement with another woman about each eating their children in turns for food during the famine. According to the complainant, she has given up her child and had been eaten, but the other woman was reluctant to give up her child to be eaten by the agreement. Upon hearing the complaint the king tore his clothes because he had been confronted with the gravity of the situation; Samaria was in for the first time on a higher level.

The problem was that when the other woman's son has been eaten, the woman refused to bring herself to bear that her son is going to be killed and be eaten like the other woman's son. So this was what brought the issue to the king. The point that I am trying to make is the fact that the Syrian army never came to the city with their bows and arrows or guns yet they were killed. Even though, they were not the ones who were killing these women children, yet they were killing themselves. You have been besieged when you self-destruct, or you have the tendency to self-destruct. What do I mean by that? When you have the tendency to develop certain attitudes and habits that you know it will destroy you and yet those habits or attitudes cannot be checked or adequately dealt with, then have been besieged. Anytime that you have that self-destructive tendencies that this thing I am doing will kill me yet you keep on doing then you have been besieged.

Some say, "I am sleeping too much", and it will leave me poor; I am eating junk food it will kill and you keep on eating. Some Christian doctors counsel the patients with the diseases that they risk their lives of if they take in too much fat or alcohol or smoke yet they themselves are alcoholics or chain smokers. You have to understand that you have been besieged. You are not free when you cannot do what you think is right. Whatever the roots of your self-destructive behavior may be, identifying and dealing with them will do you a world of good and make the process much more effective and sustainable.

Difficulty Believing in God's Word

At the peak of the famine, when people were eating one another for food, all hope was lost and a prophet arose and spoke the mind of God. Elisha spoke of a change that was coming within the space of 24 hours. Due to the enormity of the problem confronting them, it was almost impossible to think about such a turnaround of events within that short space of time. As a result of the prevailing circumstances, the prophet's word was openly rejected and despised. The rejection and ridicule of the word of the Lord and disbelief were sown into the hearts by a special advisor to the king. It is probably a disappointment in God for the fact that He probably allowed such a difficult situation to befall them and also for the fact that, Elisha may be making mockery of their predicament.

When you cannot believe the word of Lord anymore, it's a dangerous situation to be in. More often than not, it is characterised by the sense of justification because you might have almost certainly waited on the Lord for a long time without any solution. You might have probably been diagnosed with an incurable disease and feel the word of assurance for your divine healing seems to make a mockery of the situation.

Anytime anyone speaks the word of God it sounds in your ear like a con man's word or as though someone is making a mockery of your personal situation, it is a sign the enemy is up to something sinister. There are notwithstanding instances where people go to a particular church upon a friend's invitation and the Word of the Lord being preached speaks directly to this guests' situation and they say the one that invited them have leaked information about them to the pastor. When you moan, when you hear we should love one another, pay tithe or even to perform some act of Christian responsibility, then it is possible that you are besieged.

The truth is that the moment you say some of these things, know that you have been besieged, you are not of yourself. Because there is only one enemy to the truth and that is the devil. Anytime you have anything that counters the truth in your ears, you are not of yourself; you are not the one speaking; the enemy is lurking around that environment, and you have to be ware. Never say you are spiritual, even Peter spoke what the devil wanted to speak. Jesus said in three days time I will die but Peter said you are not dying today or tomorrow; it is a disbelief which is a sign of a siege.

"Then Peter took him, and began to rebuke him, saying, Be it far from thee, Lord: this shall not be unto thee.

But he turned, and said unto Peter, Get thee behind me, Satan: thou art an offence unto me: for thou savourest not the things that be of God, but those that be of men. Then said Jesus unto his disciples, If any man will come after me, let him deny himself, and take up his cross, and follow me.

For whosoever will save his life shall lose it: and whosoever will lose his life for my sake shall find it." (Matthew 16:22-25)

The above scripture shows how Satan wanted to use Peter to besiege Jesus Christ. Even Peter did not know the thing he was saying; it was Satan who was allowing him to say those things. So anytime there is something to counter what God had said or what God is saying to you, remember that is the devil the voice that you are hearing can never be the voice of God.

How many times have you not been spoken to by God through the pages of the bible and you told yourself "as for this prophecy I have heard it and I want to hear something different". This has been the reaction of people to God's Word and had as a result missed out on the blessings of God and also opened the door to the enemy to afflict them. Unbelief is when you make up your own mind about what God can and cannot do or what God will not do and how He does and does not operate. It is malfunction in our operational response to God's Word because through faith, you could see the manifestation of God's presence in your life.

"Now faith is the substance of things hoped for, the evidence of things not seen. For by it the elders obtained a good report. Through faith we understand that the worlds were framed by the word of God, so that things which are seen were not made of things which do appear." (Hebrews 11:1-3)

The interpretation of the scriptures quoted above is that the demonstration of faith in God would mean to believe and to do what His Word says even when it is contrary to the prevailing circumstances of your life.

The moment you begin to doubt God; you are besieged. You may think you are justifying or behaving as if God must stop talking and start doing it in your life, but you do not know that you have been besieged. You may even be angry, God should have shown up earlier, but you need to understand that God is not at any time late. And God will never do anything without first of all sending forth His word. So when you reject His word, you have rejected His presence in your life and the manifestation of that which He has spoken.

That is why when the Angel appeared unto Mary and Mary asked the question how could these things be? And the Angel said the power of the Most High shall overshadow you when you get pregnant with the baby and the child you shall give birth to shall be called Emmanuel who shall be the deliverer of His people. And do you know what Mary said; do it unto me according to your word. So if at any time, you reject the Word of the Lord, you have to understand it is to your enemy's advantage. You are giving him the advantage to afflict you more.

We have to be able to take these things and keep them in our hearts because the word when you stand against it, anything that stands against it would be overridden by the power of the word. The word of God says where there is the word there is power.

The king who Elisha gave the prophecy to, thought Elisha was out of his mind when he said food was going to be sold very cheap because it could not make sense at the time. This clearly demonstrates how a person who hears the word and does not believe and also stands up against it. It is the truth that anything that stands up against the Word of the Lord is overridden by the power inherent in the Word. All things shall pass away, but the Word of God shall abide forever.

In spite of the challenges that confront you, do not be offended by the Word of the Lord. It is the starting point for every genuine work of God in the life of the believer. In John 1:1-3, He would not do anything without the word. Inasmuch as we may seek signs and wonders, these signs and wonders may have no basis on the Word of God. Therefore, we need to embrace the Word of the Lord and to wait on the Lord patiently to make his Word flesh in our lives, as a replacement of our challenges and difficulties.

Taking Out your Frustrations on the Wrong People

An interesting situation occurred at the peak of the famine that plagued the city of Samaria. After the king has had the difficult encounter with the woman who appealed to him for arbitration in the case of her agreement with the other woman to eat their children, he was overcome with grief that grief resorted to anger against God's spokesperson and prophet. He vowed to kill Elisha because it was his presence in their city that the calamity had befallen them.

Furthermore, he felt since Elisha prophesied for God, should he hurt Elisha, he was indirectly hurting God because for him, God was the cause of what they were going through. Have you ever imagined why Satan hates you so much always looking for ways to bring you down? His mission the bible says is to steal, kill and destroy. Satan besieges us, plots evil for us, lays snares, lies in wait for the people of God because we are in the image of God. We are God's vice regents here on earth and so if he could destroy us, he knows how much God would be hurt by that. Just think about this; why didn't Satan go to God to confront Him about the lies, he supposed God had told to Adam and Eve? Why did he have to come to Adam and Eve? It was because he was telling lies about the instructions, God gave to Adam and Eve in the garden and also because he didn't have the authority and power enough to fight God. After all, wasn't Satan much older than Adam and Eve and existed many years before Adam and Eve came to live in the garden. The only way he could get to hurt God was to attempt to get Adam and Eve on his side in rebellion against God, to make nonsense of what God had made mankind to be; His image and likeness.

It is often the case that when you take your frustrations out on your spiritual leader or people or things, which are not the cause of your problems or troubles, then you are besieged. It is also a tactic the enemy uses to cause you to lose focus on him as the author of all forms of evil. When you take your frustration on your spiritual leader is a sign that you have been besieged. Elisha was sitting around the house with his elders deliberating on some important issues but when the king heard that people were killing their own children, he became worried and sent for Elisha for his head to be cut off.

Was Elisha the problem? Did Elisha cause the problem or the famine? Who was the problem? The Syrian Army was the problem but the king did not go to the Syrian camp to cut off their heads. This is a sign of been besieged because he took his frustration to the wrong person.

Sometimes, people might come to you and tell you a whole lot of stories about those God has set over your soul in your church and ministry and based upon the pictures painted to you, you may jump into conclusion to blame certain people who might not have anything to do with the problem. I have heard stories where people have left churches because some evil befell them, and they felt if their pastor or minister was anointed enough they might have escaped that challenge. One thing to understand is that, God plants each and everyone in different churches assuming the assignment he has given to that particular leader of the church, to be able to nurture you into growth and maturity. Therefore, not every individual will do well in any church at all. You have to have been planted in a specific church by the Lord to receive the right amount of spiritual nourishment to grow.

In the same way as certain plants need a precise soil type and even a particular climatic condition so is the believer in Christ. You can't just be planted anywhere and expect to do well. Therefore, the strategy of the enemy as in the story from 2 Kings 6 is to besiege you and push you into thinking that your predicament is as a result of your minister or pastor then cause you to move out of the church. Thereby cutting yourself as a member of that local body of Christ which the minister or pastor is the head. When you do, you have cut off the grace that must flow from the head through the beard to reach you.

"How good and pleasant it is when God's people live together in unity!" (Psalm 133:1)

The oil was poured upon the head of Aaron and it went to his beard and through to the hem of his garment. The oil is always poured upon the head. Therefore, if you dishonour the head, or you detached yourself from the head when the oil is poured, it will not reach you. Trying to encourage people to do evil, rebel and take a course of action detrimental to the stability of the local body of Christ, yet they have thought they were fighting the minister or the pastor. In the end, they have left the church in huge numbers and some of them have withered and died along the way.

When you detach yourself and the oil never gets to you that is how the devil hung people dry. They can be sitting close to something that is beneficial to anybody, and yet they will not benefit from it. They become complainants and saboteurs, and therefore, do not benefit from the set man of the house God has planted them. The answer is because they have detached themselves from the head and as a result they are not getting the oil that is supposed to be flowing into their lives to make life better.

We can learn a very good lesson from David at the time when he was being pursued by King Saul, he had the opportunity to kill Saul at an unexpected time, but he did not, he said it was not in his place to destroy the Lord's anointed. He didn't want to contravene the laws because he knew whatever he did was going to come back to haunt him some day so why do it. There wouldn't have been any rebuke or backlash from his men or the whole of Israel because it was a situation of warfare, and they knew that Saul after the life of David. It would have also served as a quicker way to get David to the throne, but he refused to employ his own means. He still recognised Saul as his king, and ruler over God's people. Examining how David handled such matters, I conclude the perfect condition of his heart endeared him to God. David had his own shortcomings and weaknesses, but he understood spiritual protocol.

Let us be careful when people come with such stories; just tell them, I am not interested in such stuff, if you want to talk about this, then find another address. Nevertheless, most of us have never been bold enough to turn people away for evil because we want people to like us. We say if I tell him or her to go away with his or her story, then how am I going to make another friend and after all, he or she is my friend, but we must tell the people as it is.

Elisha did not do anything wrong but the king was seeking his head; the king should have gone to the Syrian army because they have besieged the city but he took out his frustration on Elisha because he was the easy target to deal with. We have situations in our churches, homes, and work. Sometimes, people think the pastor or the father or the manager or the child is the easy target.

Let us learn to divert our frustrations to the right place or person. I think the only person we must first direct our situation, especially when it comes to spiritual warfare is the God Almighty. A leader or a pastor in your church is, however, there to help you carry your burdens but if, for some reason, you didn't get answers to your prayers, or you are frustrated by the turn of events, do not take out on them. Go to them humbly and ask them to keep bearing you up in prayer.

I can recall particular instances when people on particular national assignments such as playing in their national football teams have performed badly, or let their nation down, some of their family members have been threatened by certain unscrupulous persons and even tried to burn down their houses. A member of a national football team, who played in defence got shot and killed in his homeland after the team, lost their game to another country through a defensive blunder. They took their frustrations to his family members and his houses, which were neither the cause nor the solution to the issue that was at stake.

In the same way, when some parents have challenges at their work places or when they pray and yet their problems are not solved, they turn to blame their grandmothers of witchcraft or even hit their children at the least of offence committed.

The point that I am trying to make is that do not take out your frustrations on other people such as your leaders because of what they are doing or what they are not doing; they are not the cause of the trouble. There is only one person who makes sure your life is miserable, the devil. Always attack the devil that is the cause of your problem rather than people who do not matter in your problem.

Certainly, there is no human being which is your enemy; the devil is. See beyond even the human characters involved and arm yourself for war against the enemy behind the scenes. Sometimes too, people begin to seek short cut means of lessening their frustration, which would end up compounding the problem. People have resorted to drugs and alcohol, for instance, in dealing with their problems, instead of tackling the root of the frustration. Others do not want to hear even the name of God or have anything to do with God because something dreadful happened; God is not the author of evil. Running away from God in anger for something awful that happened to you in life is like taking out your frustration of the incident on an all-merciful God.

Cannot Pray as Before

It is obvious that God is reached through prayer, and the king knew that too well. There have been instances throughout the history of Israel where kings have enquired of God the direction to take in matters of national importance such as the current crisis. The King should have resorted to prayer to seek God on behalf of the land or should have consulted the prophet to seek direction of God on behalf of the nation.

Unfortunately, he somewhat made the prophet the target of his frustration. It is obvious that the besiegement of the Syrian army and the threat of internal self-destruction has made the king lose faith in God and was very angry at God.

It is the case that when you are not motivated to pray consistently in any situation, you find yourself then you are besieged.

There have been times throughout my life when I have been up and down, times when prayer seems to come easy, and times when prayer does not come easy at all because you are weighed down by the problems and challenges that surround you. I have heard people speak about getting on their knees to pray and having the feeling that their prayers were bouncing off the ceiling, going no higher than the ceiling, that nobody was hearing it but them. They do not think God is actually hearing what they are saying. The truth is that they are so much swamped with their own problems that they cannot believe God hears them. The reason I say this is because we connect to God by faith and whether you feel your prayer has been heard or not should not stop you from praying. As a matter of fact, God hears our prayers. It is often our minds that play tricks on us other than God not hearing us when we pray.

If you find yourself in this situation, or you consider prayer as a long way to get your problem solve because God might not fast track the response of your prayers, then you are besieged. God is always near. Have you considered that God even hears the prayer of sinners to save them? God had to listen to you when you prayed the sinner's prayer and surrounded your life to Him. No prayer goes unnoticed in the sight of God.

In the early days of the church, Paul and Silas held bound in prison, prayed until the building shook for them and prisoners in that same prison to be released. Moses prayed, and as long as his hands were held up, Israel won the war. The moment his hands came down, Israel lost the war. The point is this, the moment you stop praying, you would be losing your battle in the besiegement. Your prayer is the secret of releasing God's power in your life. Jesus had a powerful prayer life; He prayed all night. And after he had prayed all night, then came the signs and wonders. This world will do everything in its power to crowd out the truly significant things in your life. What could be more significant than being able to talk to the God of the entire universe, and be heard, and have Him respond? And yet, it is so easy for us to find things that are more important than that to us at the moment.

Let us know that the devil came to steal, kill and destroy (John 10:10); he does everything possible to besiege you from taking prayer seriously. If you feel it important to sleep or go round the wash room or time to get yourself busy about other things when it time to pray, remember the devil is using those alternative activities as a besiegement tactics. It is through prayer that you get strengthened in the spiritual warfare, ask from God whatever you desire but the devil has brainwashed many not to value that moment of prayer.

CHAPTER FOUR

HOW DO YOU BREAK THE SIEGE?

The building of the siege by the enemy creates a truly difficult situation and as discussed in the preceding chapter can lead to certain decisions and actions taken by the one who has been besieged with consequences that can be extremely dire. In spite of the grim picture that can be painted of the results and effects of a siege, sieges can be broken. In the narrative, the siege was broken by four lepers determination and through a supernatural initiative of God. We would look for the sequence of events prior to and during the breaking of the siege. We would draw lessons and inferences from these acts and events.

You need a Prophetic Word

The whole process of liberation from the military siege against Samaria begun with the Prophet Elisha declaring the mind of God about the situation the people found themselves in.

You, first of all, need a prophetic word to hang on. You do not only break a siege by fasting and prayers, but you need a word to hang on. Prayer based on emotions and feelings does not accomplish anything. What I mean by a prophetic word is not exclusively a word that has been prophesied about your life but the word you read and hear daily that speaks to your relevant circumstances.

One thing we need to get clearly in our understanding is that Jesus Christ died for all humans but when we accept Christ as our Lord and personal saviour, we enter a personal relationship with Him on a basis of a covenant sealed by His blood. He now lives forever making intercession for us, on the right-hand side of God the father for us, but we are still able to relate to him by faith through His word. The bible has been around for so many years and many people own one, but once you accept Jesus Christ as

Lord and saviour, the bible ceases to be a public book but the Word of the Lord to you personally. Therefore, your relationship with Christ is lived through the Word because He is one with his Word (John 1:1-14). Consequently, the scripture is the Word of the Lord to you. Let us discuss our relationship to the Word of the Lord into much detail in the paragraphs below.

In the New Testament, the Greek words logos and rhema are both translated word of God. Logos is generally used to refer to the totality of the Word of God as well as the person of Jesus Christ, Who is the living Logos.

"The seed is the Word [logos] of God" (Luke 8:11). "Holding forth the word [logos] of life" (Philippians 2:16). "Rightly dividing the word [logos] of truth" (II Timothy 2:15). *"For the word [logos] of God is quick, and powerful"* (Hebrews 4:12).

"Being born again, not of corruptible seed, but of incorruptible, by the word [logos] of God" (I Peter 1:23). *"As newborn babes, desire the sincere milk of the word [logikos, from logos], that ye may grow thereby"* (I Peter 2:2).

Scripture uses the Greek word *rhema* to refer to the spoken word given by a living voice and is used to describe a particular message that was given to individuals for their personal application. The following passages are examples of this:

- Jesus told Peter he would deny Him—*"Peter remembered the word [rhema] of Jesus, which said unto him, Before the cock crow, thou shalt deny me thrice"* (Matthew 26:75).

- The angel told Mary that she would have a child—*"Mary said, Behold the handmaid of the Lord; be it unto me according to thy word [rhema]"* (Luke 1:38).

- Simeon was told he would see Christ before he died—*"Now lettest thou thy servant depart in peace, according to thy word [rhema]"* (Luke 2:29).

- God gave John the message he was to preach as a forerunner to Christ—*"The word [rhema] of God came unto John"* (Luke 3:2).

- Jesus told Peter where to cast his nets—*"Master, we have toiled all the night, and have taken nothing: nevertheless at thy word [rhema] I will let down the net"* (Luke 5:5).

- God reminded Peter of His Word—*"Then remembered I the word [rhema] of the Lord, how that he said, John indeed baptized with water; but ye shall be baptized with the Holy Ghost"* (Acts 11:16).

Even in the process for a person coming to the saving knowledge of the Lord Jesus to be saved, it takes the Rhema. As some of you might have experienced, prior to being born again, you might have heard the Word of God preached so many times and yet you were not moved to accept Christ as Lord and personal saviour. Until a particular time the Word of the Lord – the Rhema, gripped you. Those who hear the Gospel receive a special message from the Holy Spirit, for no man can call Jesus Lord, but by the Holy Spirit. *"No man can say that Jesus is the Lord, but by the Holy Ghost"* (I Corinthians 12:3). Therefore, it is appropriate for the message of salvation to be a *rhema*.

Rhemas are not separate from Scripture, but a part of the whole of God's Word. In layman's terms, the Rhema is the voice behind the Word. You may read the scriptures generally but there are portions of scriptures that seem to jump out of the page to you that speak to a specific situation in your life or instructs you to take a particular decision; this is the Rhema. In other words, it is the particular appropriation of God's Word in a time and season with relevance to a distinct situation at a particular time by the Holy Spirit to an individual. Having said that every word of God is inspired, and "all scripture is given by inspiration of God, and is profitable for doctrine, for reproof, for correction, for instruction in righteousness" (II Timothy 3:16). It is the Holy Spirit Who illuminates particular Scriptures for application in a daily walk with the Lord.

The words of Jesus are significant on this point. *"Man shall not live by bread alone, but by every word [rhema] that proceedeth out of the mouth of God"* (Matthew 4:4). Jesus also stated, *"The words [rhema] that I speak unto you, they are spirit, and they are life"* (John 6:63).

This understanding of *rhema* has allowed many to apply the promise of John 15:7–8 and experience marvellous results from it. *"If ye abide in me, and my words [rhema] abide in you, ye shall ask what ye will, and it shall be done unto you. Herein is my Father glorified, that ye bear much fruit; so shall ye be my disciples."*

What we have been saying in the previous paragraph is that, there are times when you take your bible, and you are reading, a particular word speaks to you as though it knew your problem and sometimes too at church when you have been preached to, a message hits you as though the preacher knows your problem, that is the rhema.

This is the prophetic word, which you need to hang on in order to break any siege in which you may find yourself. So you need to contact the logos first in order to have a rhema. An effective prayer begins with praying the Word of God. God is under obligation to honour His Word even above His name, therefore, if you bring His Word back to Him with conviction, He will answer and send you help. You need a word from the Lord to hold on to in order to confront a siege. It is important to understand that God does nothing without His Word; therefore, His Word precedes His actions.

You can tell God that what is happening in your life does not conform to His word so you can decree and claim that you deserve the right portion that you deserve so you need a word to hang on because wherever there is the word, there is power.* Do not wait for a prophecy in your life before any siege can be broken because God will never do anything without the word (John 1:1-3).

Since sieges or strongholds are built upon lies that we have been fed, the way to tear them down is by feeding on the truth (in God's Word), which is the opposite of what the enemy has been feeding us. If the enemy has been feeding us a lie, we need to stop eating the lie and start feeding ourselves the truth. The weapon we use to tear down strongholds is found in Ephesians 6:17, *"...the sword of the Spirit, which is the word of God."* A sword is an offensive weapon and is meant to tear down and destroy the enemy's troops. Deceptions are the devil's assets in war, and he uses them against us. Take up the sword of the Spirit (God's Word) today, and start slaughtering the enemy's assets that he's been using against you!

In John 8:31-36, Jesus tells us that we can be held in bondage due to strongholds in our lives. And His solution was to, *"continue in my word... and ye shall know the truth, and the truth shall make you free."* (v. 32-32) Strongholds are torn down as we meditate on God's Word, which is truth!

A Chinese Apostle, Nee Shu-tsu (Watchman Nee) in his book "The Release of the Spirit," consistently made the point, that the outer man—the flesh must be broken for the Spirit within to be released outside.

The word of God is such that it acts like a supernatural hammer that breaks the resistance of the flesh into pieces. And so does the Word deal with every siege and resistance to your freedom, growth, expansion and upliftment. God created the world through the word, and that is why when you believe that there is a prophet in the house, you can go before the lord with His word, and you will see the manifestation in your life because God will honour his word.

You need to be determined

It seems as though it was the four lepers at the gates of Samaria, who took the prophecy Elisha gave seriously. It is probable that after the challenge of the prophecy of Elisha by the king's butler many might have dismissed the whole content of the prophecy as impossibility. Others who believe might also not know how this was going to come about and may have been waiting on the Word. At this point, the narrative focuses on the four lepers who had their homes in the outskirts of the city because of the disease which according to the Mosaic Law made them unclean to freely move around the city.

The lepers were faced with the same challenges as those in the city and probably even more but at some point, they had to confront their situation and made a decision.

Do you remember what the four lepers did? They told themselves or convinced themselves that this venture that we want to undertake is a very dangerous venture; it is 50/50 either we go the camp and be killed, or we stay here and die of hunger; all die be die, so let us decide that we are going to the camp, if we die, we die, if we live, we live. That is how we are supposed to tackle the devil and the siege in our lives. Complains like if it were not the demonic opposition in your house by now your life would have been better is not the solution. Remember that the demons have taken the battle with all their strength because their time is very short

"... Woe to the inhabiters of the earth and of the sea! for the devil is come down unto you, having

great wrath, because he knoweth that he hath but a short time." (Revelation 12:12)

We do all kinds of things but we never tackle the siege. Some even say if I were in a different church that the pastor was a prophet by now my life would have been better off. This is not the resolution of a person who is determined to make it at all cost – to see the manifestation of what the Lord has said in their lives. It is about time you came to a point that you tell yourself, you are not crossing to the following month or year with the same-old problem.

You must have a determination to beat the siege at all cost. The lepers said if we die, we die, if we live, we live, therefore, let us arise and go to the enemies' camp. Let us have that attitude that we are going to the enemies' camp to take what is ours. Some seemingly simple and unimportant decisions have great consequences. When decisions are taken in fear, unbelief, or because of negative reaction, revenge and frustration, we may unknowingly be committing spiritual suicide. Every decision should be taken in faith. There will be no regrets when we take all our decisions based on God's Word. Let's go off the fear of failure and step out to confront your siege.

That was the attitude of Shadrack, Meshach and Abednego. They told themselves that they were bowing down before the image because their God will be able to save them.

I have now understood why people do sleep during prayer times even when they are confronted with problems; they have no determination whatsoever to get rid of their problems. God needs some cooperation from you to solve the problem for you. To break the siege, you need to build a determination to end the siege based on faith in God's Word and take the necessary actions in line with that. There are times when we are not sure if our efforts would be worthwhile. We are afraid to put in all those emotional, spiritual, mental energy, just in case we end up failing to get the required results.

Even so, we need to come to that place where we will be determined to say whether the problem is big or small, whether it looks possible or not, once God has spoken; I am ready to move forward.

The God that we serve is bigger than any problem and any siege built around your life to limit you and cause you grief. Therefore, we are supposed to face problems with courageous words of the lepers, if we die, we die, and if we live we live, similar to what the three young men said to Nebuchadnezzar, we won't bow because our God can save us, and even if He doesn't in this particular instance we won't bow anyway.

When we make the determination to simply live life according to God's plan, the end result will always be a victory! The path to victory as a believer is to be determined to follow God's plan and walk with Him. We just need to be patient, consistent, and determined to walk with God and carry out His business, His way.

This same principle will work when it comes to the success of our life and the church. For us to walk in victory as a church, we simply need to determine that we will do it God's way.

- We need to determine that we will adopt the Bible as the sole standard for our faith and practice.

- We need to determine that we will walk in love both to those in the church and those outside the church.

- We need to determine that we will give faithfully to support the church.

- We need to determine that we will faithfully support the worship and the work of the church.

- We need to determine that we will take advantage of every opportunity to share the message of the Gospel with a lost and dying world.

- We need to determine that we will come to the Lord's house with excitement in our hearts, to worship the Redeemer, Who died to save us from our sins and from the wrath of God.

Let me finally share with you a story of determination of one of the determined architects of the 19th century. 'In 1883, a creative engineer named John Roebling was inspired by an idea to build a spectacular bridge connecting New York with the Long Island.

However, bridge building experts throughout the world thought that this was an impossible feat and told Roebling to forget the idea. It just could not be done. It was not practical. It had never been done before. Roebling could not ignore the vision he had in his mind of this bridge. He thought about it all the time, and he knew deep in his heart that it could be done. He just had to share the dream with someone else. After much discussion and persuasion, he managed to convince his son Washington, an up-and-coming engineer, that the bridge, in fact, could be built. Working together for the first time, the father and son developed concepts of how it could be accomplished and how the obstacles could be overcome.

With great excitement and inspiration, and the headiness of a wild challenge before them, they hired their crew and began to build their dream bridge. The project started well, but when it was only a few months underway, a tragic accident on the site took the life of John Roebling. Washington was also injured and left not being able to talk or walk.

"We told them so." "Crazy men and their crazy dreams." "It's foolish to chase wild visions." Everyone had a negative comment to make and felt that the project should be scrapped since the Roeblings were the only ones who knew how the bridge could be built. In spite of his handicap, Washington was never discouraged and still had a burning desire to complete the bridge, and his mind was still as sharp as ever. He tried to inspire and pass on his enthusiasm to some of his friends, but they were too daunted by the task.

As he lay on his bed in his hospital room, with the sunlight streaming through the windows, a gentle breeze blew the flimsy white curtains apart, and he could see the sky and the tops of the trees outside for just a moment.

It seemed that there was a message for him not to give up. Suddenly, an idea hit him. All he could do was move one finger and he decided to make the best use of it. By moving this, he slowly developed a code of communication with his wife. He touched his wife's arm with that finger, indicating to her that he wanted her to call the engineers again. Then he used the same method of tapping her arm to tell the engineers what to do. It seemed foolish but the project was under way again. For 13 years Washington tapped out his instructions with his finger on his wife's arm, until the bridge was finally completed. Today the spectacular Brooklyn Bridge stands in all its glory as a tribute to the triumph of one man's indomitable spirit and his determination not to be defeated by personal limitations and personal circumstances.

When we are faced with obstacles in our day-to-day life, we should remember to demonstrate a determined attitude that achieves an unachievable goal. The Brooklyn Bridge shows us that dreams that seem hopeless can be realised with determination and persistence, no matter what the odds are.'

You need to locate yourself in the Scheme of God's plans

The lepers knew straight away that they were limited in breaking the siege. Let's not view these lepers as some military strategists determined to break the siege at all cost. They were motivated by their need to fill their stomachs and not to die of hunger. They believed the Word of the Lord spoken by the prophet Elisha for themselves, and although they are not sure what the outcome could be, they were still determined to get food for themselves. It was either their personal quest or search for food would turn into a personal disaster or a national triumph. They did not care much about what would happen to them but they were optimistic of the possibility of, they having something to eat. It seems as though there was an alignment of the word spoken by the prophet and the time they found themselves talking to each other at twilight.

Destiny was knocking on the door for something extreme to unfold in their lives that would affect the fortunes of the entire nation. They were on the verge of something pronounced although they were not so sure, but they would be moved to the end to take a step which ended up being the right step. Destiny comes calling to us all the time and we would need to be able to locate yourself within God's scheme of things to fully take advantage of any situation. Think about one of the men crucified alongside Jesus Christ that Friday on Calvary. Destiny came calling out to him – he knew he was bad anyway, he was also going to die anyway and might have heard about this Jesus if not even seen him before their crucifixion, but he took his chance right there not to miss heaven by expressing belief in Jesus as the son of God.

One of the essentials of locating one's self in God's scheme of things is to be able to totally surrender our all into the hands of God. To some extent, the lepers surrendered to God because they were not ignorant of the imminent danger of the Syrian army who had camped outside the city. At every point of surrender to God, HE takes over what is left irrespective of the limitations associated with it and does something of significance with it. The result was that God amplified the sound of their footsteps, and the enemy fled leaving behind food and other important articles, which was very useful to a nation that had been under such military attack for a long time.

Similarly, during the marching round the walls of Jericho, the Israelites kept going in their dedication until they passed from the realm of their own power, into the realm of the power of God! After marching around that city seven times, they would have been too exhausted to fight! When they came into the place where they could not, but knew he could, a miracle took place and the walls around the city came tumbling down.

Let us remember that victory over our walled cities will most likely come when we get into the place where the victory is totally out of our hands and in His alone! When we get away from the realm of our ability and move beyond the realm of God's ability; then we will see what God can bring to pass in a life wholly dedicated to Him! If we want to achieve victory over the strongholds in our lives, we must realise that we lack the power to make such a victory a reality! The only way we will ever achieve victory over the walled cities in our life is for us to dedicate ourselves wholly to the will of the Lord. We must surrender ourselves completely to Him, His Word and His will. We must give up all rights to our own lives, and place everything we have and everything we are in the mighty hands of the Lord.

Locating yourself in God's scheme of things through a total surrender to Him, is the key to walking in spiritual victory. Until we are ready to sell out completely, and do it God's way with determination and dedication, we will always be prone to fail. Nevertheless, when we do it His way, we are guaranteed to cast down all the sieges in our lives.

You need to have a great heart

Here are lepers who are rejected and neglected by society because of a defect in their lives. They were more or less confined to the outskirts of the city and when there was the need at all to come into the city, they had to announce their presence by ringing bells and shouting out that they were lepers deliberately for people to stay away from them and not make contact. The reason was because it was believed that leprosy was a medical condition that was communicable and also because it was often a result of a curse from God upon a person or a family. It would have been understandable for these lepers to be bitter when they chose to but not these particular four lepers.

When they broke out into the enemy's camp after God had given them the breakthrough, they took care of their personal needs but somewhere along the line, they remembered their place in God's scheme of things that what they were doing was not good. They had not only been given access by God to this great provision which the enemy army has left behind, but they were conduits through whom salvation would come to the whole nation. They saw straight away that God's word spoken through the prophet was unfolding through them, and they could no longer play little but focusing on their personal needs alone. At that point, they informed the king and consequently, there was a rush to the enemy's camp to collect what God had provided to the nation according to the promise he made earlier.

The focus of this particular section and what we learn from these lepers was that although society as a whole had neglected them and somehow ostracised them, they maintained a pure heart. They were not out there for revenge on those who had treated them badly for the years they were ill. They did not just build their camp in the fields and stayed there with their hoard. They were such open-hearted people who wanted to please God and not to take vengeance of some sort in their own hands. They didn't see the breakthrough as a personal breakthrough but a national breakthrough. There were a few possible actions these lepers could have taken which they did not. They could have built a camp and carried everything into those camps and sold them put one item after the other to the populace and could have greatly enriched themselves as a result.

They could have also used that a bargaining power for a change of law to allocate them a permanent residence in the city, or possibly bargain for a political position at the city gate because the whole land was famished and could have done anything possible to get out of that situation. Remember that they were eating cow dung and bird droppings were being sold; others signed contracts to eat their children and so on so anything was a possibility, but they had a good heart. They recognised the event as having been triggered by God and was in no way willing to stand in the place of God or take advantage of the situation to enrich themselves or gain honour for themselves. As a matter of fact, the writer did not even bother to give the names of those four lepers, although it was through them that such a great work had been done through them.

In our day and in our times, we see people taking the glory of God for themselves when God used them to accomplish a great feat. It is understandable that he that watered is watered, as in a conduit that carries water, the conduits would come into contact with the water. Men and women who want to be used by God are to bear in mind that God would use them to accomplish great things, but it should not be a bargaining power for social status, money and riches, fame and popularity. It should not also come as a means to prove that one is important. There are a lot of in-fighting, hatred, jealousy and envy in the body of Christ and even more seriously among men and women of God because the condition of the heart is just not right.

Since many have reduced their calling and mandate of Christ to the ministry to building personal kingdoms, the values of the kingdom have been trampled and despised. There is no fulfilment in the lives of some ministers, and this has led to greed because it no longer about the one who calls – Jesus Christ but about personal kingdoms. The four lepers located themselves in God's scheme of things and they made the decision to maintain a good heart towards God and the entire society.

Willingness to Pay with Your Life

The question I asked as I studied the scriptural text was, 'were they really willing to die for what they wanted?' And the answer is yes because it was a statement they made. Their determination has not blinded them from what could happen; they knew exactly the risks involved in their actions and should anything go wrong, what the repercussions could be. They were willing to pay with their lives if that was what it took.

Similar to the four lepers at the gate of Samaria, you must have the willingness to pay for your life as a sacrifice. You must be ready to die or live.

There was a man in the early fifteen century called Hernán Cortés. He was a Spanish conquistador who led a group, an army at the peak of the Spanish empire for the purpose of annexing other nations to expand the Spanish Kingdom and influence around the world. Cortés, an army general of the Spanish army went to Mexico which was then known as the Aztec empire with about 200 soldiers in a small ship.

Upon arrival, he ordered the soldiers to remove all that they brought which were inside the ship out and place them at the seashore. He ordered the ship to be set on fire and indeed the ship was burnt into ashes. He then announced to his comrades that the ship that brought us from Spain to this Aztec empire has been burnt so we are left with two choices; either we conquer the army of the Aztec empire and inhabit the land or we die.

This made about 200 soldiers to conquer an empire of about two million people with an army of about 300,000. This is because they realised that there was no turning back; either they fight and win, or they give up and die. This is the attitude that we need to develop. The demons in your house, tell yourself that it is either they die, or you die. You must always tell yourself that either you die, or they will die. We must come to a point where we stick to winning only.

In Hernán Cortés situation, he made them aware that there is no option of running away; either we win or we die! This gallant effort by Hernán Cortés made Mexico to become a Spanish colony. In the same way, the four lepers did not offer themselves the option to retreat should something go wrong. They were willing to pay with their lives.

All the problems you are going through, you must be bold to say as for me and my house, we shall overcome them. It should not be just talk, but you must be willing and ready to work. It may not be easy, but you must be willing to work. The doors might be shut, but you have to try to find another way to get in; you must be willing and ready to give it all you've got. One of the things that rob us of our triumph and victories in life is that we sometimes hold back without giving it our all at once. We also often hide behind the guise of God taking over and sit back and watch so much happen outside the will of God. We need to put in all we can in all situations as though it all depends on us.

When Jonah decided to run from his problems, he had to pay—real cash. He paid to ride a boat headed to the opposite direction of what he thought was his problem. Nevertheless, when he runs from what he perceives as his problem, he ends up right in the middle of another problem—a violent storm at sea. The sailors aboard the ship were in of fear of their lives, and they end up throwing all their cargo overboard in an attempt to save their ship, and their lives. Jonah finally admits he is the cause of all their problems and tells them to throw him overboard (he pay the price). These blameless sailors experience a great financial loss because of Jonah's decision to run from his perceived problem of preaching to those particular people in Nineveh.

It was only when Jonah faced his problem, that the guiltless sailors experienced freedom from the damaging consequences of Jonah's disobedience. When Jonah faces his "problems"— going to preach in the city of Nineveh—a great revival comes, and thousands repent and turn to God. You must be ready to pay the price in order to stop or break any siege in your life.

Do not stand against God's Word

The leper's assessment of the grim situation of their imminent death whichever way meant that they left their ordeal and situation in the hands of God. It is possible that God could not find others within the city whom he could use because they couldn't believe the word of the Lord spoken by the prophet. The influence of those in authority and their disbelief might have negatively influenced people not to give much attention to the word of the Lord.

Unfortunately, the attempt to openly ridicule the prophet of God was met with a prophetic word that the man who openly stood against the Word of The Lord would hear and sees the fulfilment of the prophecy but would not partake in the deliverance the Lord brought upon his people. And behold at the time when the lepers came to announce the siege had been broken in the rush and scramble for food; that particular officer died in the stampede that ensued upon the announcement of the abundance of food. We need to believe in the Word of the Lord, as God does nothing without His Word. Everything God does in based on the Word. Therefore, we need to pay attention to believe in the Word of God.

The Bible tells of how Elijah was fed by the birds during a famine. Anyone with that kind of faith would stay where he was for the duration of the famine, but God impressed on him to leave for a purpose. *"The brook dried up and, one morning, the birds failed to come. Then the Lord told Elijah, Arise, get thee to Zarephath...I have commanded a widow woman there to sustain thee"* (I Kings 17:9).

God was providing that widow a chance to give to Him that He might give to her. He would ask her to give all and if she did, great blessings were to follow. The widow trusted God when Elijah said to her, *"Bring me, I pray thee, a morsel of bread in thine hand. And she said, As the Lord thy God liveth, I have not a cake, but an handful of meal in a barrel, and a little oil in a cruse: and, behold, I am gathering two sticks, that I may go in and dress it for me and my son, that we may eat it, and die"* (verse 12).

What a bleak outlook! When you are down that low, you may just as well give your last morsel to God because he can cause a turnaround. Would you have baked that cake for Elijah? Would you have given God a chance? God doesn't want you to wait until you are out of debt before you pay your tithes and give your offerings. God said if you fail in your tithes and offerings that you have robbed Him. Bring ye all the tithes...prove me now herewith, saith the Lord of hosts, if I will not open to you the windows of heaven, and pour you out a blessing, that there shall not be room enough to receive it (Malachi 3:10).

The widow woman believed Elijah when he told her what thus saith the Lord God of Israel: The barrel of meal shall not waste, neither shall the cruse of oil fail, until the day that the Lord send rain upon the earth (verse 14). That woman made a cake for Elijah first. It took great faith, for not only her life, but also the life of her son was at stake. To think that she would give that last handful of meal to the man of God rather than her own son is hard for many to imagine. When she went back to that meal barrel, it was filled and running over, the cruse of oil full, too. And *the barrel of meal wasted not, neither did the cruse of oil fail, according to the word of the Lord, which he spake by Elijah* (verse 16). It wasn't magic or luck; it came about through faith in God.

The widow's siege of acute lack in that sense was broken through faith in the anointing of God. She gave her last to God and found that she could never out–give God. The anointing in Elijah's life helped bring about deliverance for that woman. Miracle power worked in Elijah's life broke the bondage. God can work a miracle for your needs whatever they are: physical, mental, spiritual or financial.

The city of Samaria was under siege. People were starving; some were driven to the point of eating their own children. Four lepers outside the gates of Samaria were starving too, but they said, *"Why sit we here until we die?"* and started along the road for a miracle. God was going to use them. Although they had become accustomed to sitting by the gate, they had to break out of that rut before God could move for them. Maybe you've been in one place so long that it's worn into a pit that you can no longer see over; you're afraid to make a move.

Someone once said that a turtle never got anywhere unless he sticks his neck out. You can coil up in your little shell crying, "Lord, send a miracle; Lord, send a miracle!" you can stick your neck out and take a step. You do not feel like it? Have you ever seen the condition a leper gets in? I have, and I know those four leprous men didn't feel like walking down the road, but they did anyway. As they came, the Lord put great terror in the hearts of the Syrians.

The starving lepers entered the camp and had a feast. A miracle was theirs: God used them; He broke the siege. If God can use four lepers whose flesh is falling from their bodies, why can't He use you? When in sin, you were a spiritual leper; but then God cleansed you, made you a new creature in Him as you accepted Jesus into your heart. He cleansed you, and you must know that He will work a miracle for you if that is your need. We live in the day of the miraculous. God will not do the miracle in the way you want it done; He will do it His way. You have the choice of yielding to God's methods or of taking the bit in your teeth and trying to do everything for yourself.

Do you want to work where YOU want to work, or do you want to work where GOD wants you to work? Will you let God prosper you, or will you sit in one place wondering why God doesn't give the miracle? If you've prayed and prayed, done absolutely all, you know how to do, maybe it's time to step out into God's power like the lepers did. When they started walking, God prepared the way. Walk for your deliverance—why sit there until you die? If you want that siege broken, it's time to move, stop coiling up in your shell. "But things are apt to get worse," you say. Sometimes they have to get worsened before they can get better. Learn to be humble yourself before the Lord.

The prophet Elisha was approached by a woman in deep trouble. Her husband died; she had no money, and her sons were about to be sold into slavery. Elisha asked her what she had to work with. She replied, *Thine handmaid hath nothing in the house, save a pot of oil* (II Kings 4:2). Because that's all she had, she looked everywhere but the right place for a miracle. How like her we are today! If there seems to be a lot to work with, we'll believe God for a miracle. Our faith sinks, however, when we see nothing. We forget not that out of nothing God created the whole universe from. He can perform a miracle for you out of absolutely nothing! All He wants is for you to get ready, so He can use you; you are the channel He must work through you. Be ready for the faith–God to take you over. "Mould me and make me, Lord," you ask.

However, in your heart, you really think you

already have been moulded and made. It seems to be the case that whenever we feel we are moulded into just the right way, that the Lord breaks our vessel into a thousand pieces. "But I can't take any more, Lord!" you cry. The Lord promised that when things become worse than you could bear, He would provide a way of escape. If there is none, then you can bear a little more. "I can take it Lord; I can take it." He gives you grace and help for your situation.

Elisha did not do all the work for the woman who came to him for help; he gave her something to do. She was to borrow from her neighbours as many empty vessels as she could. Would you have done it? Everyone in the community knew the poor state that woman was in; they probably thought she had snapped mentally under the strain when she started collecting pots. Soon her whole house overflowed with empty vessels. The world thought she was a loser, but God looked upon her as a winner. Get ready for the blessings of God, and when they come, recognise them and hold them to your bosom.

After the woman collected all the empty vessels, Elisha told her to go inside her house and shut the door. By doing that she shut out all unbelievers. When God starts moving for you, do not tell anybody—wait for the miracle to complete before you testify. When the doubters were shut out, the power of God broke that woman's bondage. She started pouring oil into the empty vessels from her one little pot of oil. The oil kept pouring until all the empty vessels were filled. Elisha then said to her, *"Go, sell the oil, and pay thy debt, and live thou and thy children of the rest"* (II Kings 4:7).

God will move; He will supply your need if you look to Him and are obedient. Simon needed money to pay taxes, and Jesus told him go down to the sea. *"Cast an hook, and take up the fish that first cometh up; and when thou hast opened his mouth, thou shalt find a piece of money: that take, and give unto them for me and thee"* (Matthew 17:27). What fantastic ways the Lord uses to provide for His people! Would you have been obedient, had a true man of God told you to get money in that way? Some of you cannot accept the fact that God will move for you because you have not stopped worrying long enough so that faith can take over. So long as you worry; you are not accepting God's plan for your life. Get ready for God's miracle. Get ready for God to move for you; prepare for your siege to be broken, whatever it is!

You say you believe God? You do not if worry keeps you awake at night. Have you ever stayed alert at night and walked the floor because you had a good dose of faith? Too many people say, "Lord, I believe, I believe," and in the next breath ask, "What am I going to do?" That is NOT faith— faith is full assurance that God will do what He said He would do. Faith takes all the worry out. When faith comes in, fear goes out the window. You do not have to conquer worry and fear all by yourself. All you need to do is to open the door and say, "Come in faith, come on in!" When faith possesses your heart and mind, there's no room for fear.

Your little faith must grow, and it will as you trust God.

The Shield of Faith is defensive, and it enables you to extinguish the flaming missiles of Satan. Faith is simply trusting God and Faith comes by hearing, and hearing the (rhema or spoken) Word of God. Jesus told us to speak aloud directly to the situation based upon what the Word says. He said that if we do, and have faith in what the Word said, and do not doubt, that we will have whatever we say. You can praise God and give thanks for it as though it already manifested! This is not particularly easy when what you are wielding your shield of faith against a sickness or disease that is causing severe pain or discomfort, but without the shield of faith you are an open target to the enemy.

The victory of Jesus Christ is your victory. What Jesus suffered, His death, burial, resurrection and ascension to heaven is for our deliverance from the dominion of Satan and evil, and that we might be enthroned to reign in this life. I am therefore announcing this to you that your siege is over. Jesus Christ has defeated the devil already and there is no power that can stop you anymore.

"How God anointed Jesus of Nazareth with the Holy Ghost and with power: who went about doing good, and healing all that were oppressed of the devil; for God was with him." (Acts 10:38)

"You are free and cannot be stopped anymore. You have been raised to be a king here on earth that you might reign on earth and not be tied down or ruled over by the enemy." (Revelation 5:10)

"For if, by the trespass of the one man, death reigned through that one man, how much more will those who receive God's abundant provision of grace and of the gift of righteousness reign in life through the one man, Jesus Christ."
(Romans 5:17)

Being declared a king proves the believer is no longer bound or under the dominion of the devil. God did not make you a king to remain in oppression, but that you might reign.

You have to decide to reign or remain in subjection to the enemy. Do not see the devil as stronger than you. Do not see your enemies or the demonic people attacking and trying to stop you as stronger than you. Those things that have been rough and difficult with you, does not nullify the scriptures about your deliverance and enthronement. You are expected to appropriate the promises of God into your life. You are expected to enforce your freedom over the enemy and put them where they truly belong – under your feet. Get rid of the negative mentality about your situation, and cast out the enemy from your life and experience. Cast out the fear of them that has built a siege around you, for the siege is over.

God sent Jesus Christ to deliver the oppressed. In the same way, Jesus Christ sent us to deliver others who are oppressed by the devil.

All Christians must be aware that God has equipped them to overcome Satan's power. The Apostle Paul said that *"the weapons of our warfare are not carnal (of a fleshly or earthly nature), but mighty in God for pulling down strongholds"* (2 Corinthians 10:4).

This is because when the seventy disciples returned to the Lord rejoicing about the results of their ministry. They remarked, *"Lord, even the demons are subject to us in Your name"* (Luke 10:17). But then Jesus pointed out that the great marvel of this was that the devils were subject to them because their names were "written in heaven." In other words, because they were saved -- because of their relationship with Christ, they had authority over the Devil by the name of Jesus. Jesus has given all His followers -- all those who know Jesus personally as their Lord and Saviour -- the authority to use His name to expel the forces of evil. To all believers, Jesus said, *"In My name, they will cast out demons..."* (Mark 16:17).

CHAPTER FIVE

OTHERS DID IT, YOU CAN DO IT!

There has been a discussion of the various principles of breaking sieges based on the narrative in 2 Kings 6 and 7. We would look at other instances in the scriptures by application that speaks to the same effect of overcoming the attacks from the enemy.

Do not stop Praises and Worship

Praise and worship is one of the important drivers in breaking any siege in your life. Even though things are not moving along the way they should be moving yet the way to keep things moving is to praise and worship God.

When the children of Judah found themselves outnumbered by the hostile armies of Ammon,

Moab, and mount Seir, King Jehoshaphat and all the people sought the Lord for His help. The Lord assured the people that this would be His battle. He told them to go out against them, and He would do the fighting for them. So what did the children of Judah do? Being the people of "praise" (Judah actually means Praise), and knowing that God manifests His power through praise, they sent their army against their enemies, led with praises!

They went, ahead of the army declaring, "Praise the Lord, for His mercy endures forever!" And the scripture says, "...when they began to sing and to praise, the LORD set ambushments against the children of Ammon, Moab, and mount Seir, which were come against Judah; and they were smitten" (II Chronicles 20:22).

Israel used their praise and worship of the Lord as a weapon against their enemies and by doing so, God gave them the victory! This is a lesson for us today. What we must learn from this is that when we praise and worship God, he will show up in a mighty way on our behalf and help us to defeat our enemies! Although they fought a physical battle, we as believers in Christ today are fighting a spiritual battle, and as we worship him in spirit and in truth, he also gives us the assurance that we too will be victorious.

When we praise and worship God, not only do our enemies scatter but He brings great changes and transformations to our lives. Each time we come into His awesome presence, He changes us from glory to glory. He brings us healing, loving correction, solutions for our problems, peace, joy and hope. In his presence, our minds are changed, and we will be able to perceive and understand things differently. God will give us spiritual insight. We will be able to see things as God sees them. Gigantic problems are reduced to tiny ones through praise and worship. We are able to see how nothing is too hard for our Great God and how he will bring us the victory that he has already promised us in his word.

Paul and Silas knew the secret of how to lift their hearts above their troubles and enter into God's presence and power. Through praise and worship their hearts were raised into the joyous presence and peace of God, and provided God a channel for his power to operate in their circumstances.

God promises that we will not have to fight

the battle. God will fight it for us! Praise God for the victory He is going to give us. "Praise is the language of faith." When the people praised God, the Lord set ambushes to defeat the enemy. What an awesome victory!

You need to stand firm in God through prayer

Pray and seek God's face. Ask the Holy Spirit to guide and direct your prayers. Use your mouth to declare, decree and establish the authority of God's word in your life over negative spiritual influences. This means those pessimistic thoughts, feelings of jealousy, envy or revenge, you need to reject them and assert God's view on the matter instead. Paul tells Christians, to be strong in the Lord and in the power of His might. Do not do this alone, stand firm in the Lord, and He will fight the battle for you. Walk in the spirit and not in your own natural ability. The Lord will fight for you; you need only to be still. Come together with other believers to pray and intercede against strongholds until you get results. *"The Lord will fight for you; you need only to be still."* (Exodus 14:14)

There is intensified power in the gathering of

more believers. One puts away a thousand and two ten thousand. Prayer with fasting intensifies faith, and faith will break strongholds. "Then the disciples came to Jesus privately and said, "Why could we not cast him out? However, this kind does not go out except by prayer and fasting" (Matthew 17:19, 21).

The power of prayer should not be underestimated. James 5:16-18 declares, *"…The prayer of a righteous man is powerful and effective. Elijah was a man just like us. He prayed earnestly that it would not rain, and it did not rain on the land for three and a half years. Again he prayed, and the heavens gave rain, and the earth produced its crops."* God most definitely listens to prayers, answers prayers, and moves in response to prayers.

Jesus taught, *"…I tell you the truth, if you have faith as small as a mustard seed, you can say to this mountain, 'Move from here to there', and it will move. Nothing will be impossible for you"* (Matthew 17:20). 2 Corinthians 10:4-5 tells us," The weapons we fight with are not the weapons of the world. On the contrary, they have divine power to demolish strongholds. We demolish arguments and every pretension that sets itself up against the knowledge of God, and we take captive every thought to make it obedient to Christ." The Bible urges us, "And pray in the Spirit on all occasions with all kinds of prayers and requests. With this in mind, be alert and always keep on praying for all the saints" (Ephesians 6:18).

You need to increase your Faith

Allow your faith to be demonstrated in your actions. Do not just say you believe you are the righteousness of God through Christ and then when crisis hits you, you become frazzled. Let your life be faith-filled and live like you believe the words you read in your Bible. It's not about memorization; it's about revelation and transformation.

The story of Daniel in the lions' den, is one of the most dramatic incidents recorded in the Bible, is a great strengthener to faith, a challenge to stand firm in a time of testing and trial.

Your words and thoughts are containers of power. They can bring in power from the Kingdom of God or the kingdom of darkness; it's your choice. This is one of your most powerful weapons against pulling down strongholds, because the Bible says out of the abundance from the heart, the mouth speaks and also as a person thinks so is he. Change your thoughts, change your words and God's power will change your life.

Exercise the Authority

Every believer has the right to use the authority of Jesus' name to bind and take authority over Satan's activities. *"No one can enter a strong man's house and plunder his goods, unless he first binds the strong man, and then he will plunder his house"* (Mark 3:27). Issue a spoken command to the devil that he is bound and he must leave the stronghold! Exercising authority in the name of Jesus will expel the devil's influence. *"And these signs will follow those who believe: In My name they will cast out demons; they will speak with new tongues..."* (Mark 16:17).

Whenever you submit yourselves and draw close to God you can break any siege in your life. The Bible says when you draw near to God, you can resist Satan, and he will flee. The Devil runs from submitted, yielded Christians who exercise their rights in Christ and in the name of Christ. He runs from your life, and will run away from where you go. *"Therefore submit to God. Resist the devil and he will flee from you"* (James 4:7).

Let your light shine

Establish and increase the presence of God in your life. Have a life full of the awesome presence of God. Where Satan has been commanded to leave, fill it up with God's presence. Where the presence of the Lord is, the Devil cannot be there. Satan does not want to hang around where people are lifting up Jesus in worship, in singing and prayer. The presence of the Lord displaces the devil. *"For what fellowship has righteousness with lawlessness? And what communion has light with darkness?"* (2 Corinthians 6:14). This will dispel any siege that is looming or the devil wants to use as a blockade in your life.

Be always on the alert

The apostle Peter says: *"Be of sober spirit, be on the alert, for your adversary, the devil, prowls about like a roaring lion, seeking someone to devour."* (1 Peter 5:8)

To be on the alert means to be extremely watchful. We must be discerning so that we can recognise any activity of Satan. If that activity is identified early, it can be nipped in the bud. Reader, learn to see circumstances from a spiritual point of view. Things are not happening by accident. You can almost say nothing happens by accident.

Believers know that in their lives, God is working everything together for good. And of course, Satan seeks to work everything together for evil. So be on the alert and discern his activity, and then take up the Shield of Faith and the Sword of the Spirit. Be on the alert against subtle temptations. For example, the temptation to believe that the spiritual principles of warfare can be applied successfully, except in this particular case I'm facing. Alternatively, there is the temptation to think, "I've made a terrible hash of the situation. There's no hope now. I've forfeited my chances. There's no alternative left or giving up."

In times of severe combat, Satan will keep suggesting, "It does not work. It does not work." And instead of recognizing the devilish origin of these thoughts, we think that it's only our own mind telling us so. Be on the alert, particularly after any period of marked blessing. Satan must withdraw, but he will give a kick on the way out.

After we have weathered a time of crisis, we may be inclined to think things should now go smoothly. Do not forget that the enemy is persistent, and he will always seek to make a come-back.

Resist and do not Run!

Peter says, *"Your adversary, the devil, prowls about like a roaring lion, seeking someone to devour. But resist him, firm in your faith."* (1 Peter 5:8)

Satan cannot devour the believer. He can intimidate him; he can harass him; he can discourage him; he can trip him up, but he cannot devour, or destroy him, because the believer is in the hands of the Messiah. But Satan does have a lot of success through the roar he makes. In one sense, the roar of a lion never hurts anyone; however, it is possible for someone to hear the roar of the lion and drop dead from heart failure.

Now Satan is not a lion; he is a spirit being. The scriptures use the word lion as a simile to describe his nature. He is not a lion, but he goes about like a roaring lion. One of his strategies is to discourage and to cause people, especially the Lord's people, to give up. He roars, and you run. And to run away is not a good strategy by any means.

Now the tactic of Satan is to roar to stir up troubles, pressures, criticisms, accusations, problems, disturbances in any type of way, to create fear and to cause us to turn tail and run. I suppose you have been in situations like that. I have been in situations where I felt I just had to get away from it; to retreat from the battle, to give up and let whatever, have its way. Satan wants us to retreat. And tragically, his roar can cause believers to do that. Don't be intimidated by the roar of the devil!

Be Strong In The Lord

"Finally, my brethren, be strong in the Lord and in the power of His might" (Ephesians. 6:10)

You may be inclined to say, "But I am very weak." Of course you are weak! You have no spiritual strength of yourself, and if you think, you are strong of yourself, and if you think, your own physical, intellectual or persuasive power is what you use in spiritual warfare, then you have got a big defeat coming. Yes, you need to know your own weaknesses, but your favourite song should not be, "I am weak but thou art strong."

The Bible says, "Be strong in the Lord and in the power of His might." Do not harp on your own weaknesses, but become strong in the Messiah. If there is weakness, seek the Master so that He will make you mighty in spirit. Be strong in Christ!

Do not give the devil an opportunity

"Be angry, and do not sin do not let the sun go down on your wrath, nor give place to the devil." (Ephesians 4:26-27)

It is very easy to open the door to the devil. Just a few words of criticism will do it; at this moment a wrong reaction will open the door for Satan. And that's all the serpent needs. It does not need to be a big thing; even small things can open the door to the devil. Particularly, you have to watch your tongue, your emotions and your reactions. It is so common for Satan to maintain his influence over a believer by means of various mediums of temptation. The mind must decide, rationally and deliberately, to close the door to bondage, and to tie off any lose wires.

By this, I mean, if there are any objects, or any relationships that we have that are a source of temptation to us, we must reject them. Anything that causes you to stumble; anything that Satan may use to trip you up; any relationship that hinders your obedience to God, must be removed, if we avoid giving an opportunity to the devil.

Make no provision for the flesh, Paul says, to fulfil its lusts.

"But put on the Lord Jesus Christ, and make no provision for the flesh, to fulfil its lusts." (Romans 13:14)

If you want to keep the lion out, do not leave the door open. If you do not want to get an electric shock, tie off any lose wires, do not leave live wires exposed. You need to check your life and home, to see what mediums of temptation still exist. Then remove them. Any charms, or superstitious objects; anything used in occult or magic practices; any idol or object of false worship, should be disposed off. Anything that the conscience tells us is uncertain; any suspicious books or literature; any doubtful art; recordings that could have demonic influence; any CDs and videos that the conscience is uneasy about, and that could be mediums of temptation - get rid of them! Do not give the devil an opportunity to weaken you or win the spiritual battle!

Pre-empt Satan's activity

This means to hit before your enemy can hit you. *"Or how can anyone enter the strong man's house and carry of his property, unless he first binds the strong man? And then he will plunder his house."* (Mathew 12:29)

Remember the 1967, 6-day war, when Israel captured the Sinai? Trouble was brewing. Egypt, Syria and Jordan were preparing to attack Israel. Then in a brilliant move, Israel pre-empted the attack and destroyed the air-force - the planes of those three nations on the ground, before they could start. Good strategy! And we should not wait until Satan's attacks to take up our weapons.

If you are going to work for the Messiah to break the siege of the enemies, you know that Satan is going to attack. So you must pre-empt his schemes. You must take steps, beforehand, to counter his attacks. Don't fall for the temptation to think the devil is going to be kind to you. And do not try to make a bargain with him - "I will leave you alone if you leave me alone." It won't work! Even if he signed a bond, he would have no intention whatever of keeping it.

Keep Yourself in Combat-Readiness

We do not send all our cripples to the battle front, do we? We don't starve and treat our soldiers badly, so that they suffer from malnutrition or are demoralized, and then send them out. We don't give them the poorest food; we give them meat so that they will be strong. And that's what I am seeking to do in these messages - to give you some meat so that you will go out to the front, strong in the Lord. These things we are learning - the truths and principles in the Word of God, must be put into practice. Your fitness and combat-readiness will depend upon your relationship to your King, Messiah Christ.

"Fight the god fight, keeping faith and a good conscience, which some have rejected and suffered shipwreck in regard to their faith." (1Timothy 1:18-19)

"No soldier in active service entangles himself with the everyday affairs of day life, because he wants to please the one who enlisted him as a soldier." (2 Timothy 2:4)

Be Sober

Again brother, Peter says: *"Be of sober spirit, be on the alert, for your adversary, the devil, prowls about like a roaring lion"* (1 Peter 5:8). To be sober does not mean to be gloomy. True, some Christians interpret it that way; "Be gloomy!" No, the Bible is not saying be gloomy, it says, 'be sober'; and you can be filed with the joy of the Lord even while you are sober. However, if you are not sober, your mind is not under your control. When a person is drunk, you cannot get a sensible word out of him. When he/she is sober, you can talk to him rationally. We must be serious- minded because these things are vital and serious.

Do not Destroy Your Good Work

What do you think of a man who spends ten years building a beautiful house, and then dynamites the whole thing in a few minutes? And that we can destroy our work through our pride, falsehood or unwholesome talk. Wonderful works we may accomplish, and then boast about it and bring it all down. The spiritual blessing vanishes.

The prophet Malachi said, *"Cursed is the one who does the work of God deceitfully."* So whatever we do, let us not be so foolish as to attempt anything for God in a deceitful way. *"So then, putting away falsehood, speak truth, each one of you, with his neighbour, for we are members of one another . . . Let no corrupt word come out of your mouth, but only what is good and needful for building up - words that may give grace to those who hear."* (Ephesians 4:25, 29)

Do not shoot your own men

You will agree, I believe, that this is very important. Soldiers are sent out to paralyze the enemy. Of course, in some wars, soldiers take personal revenge by shooting a fellow soldier, or an officer. And unfortunately, Christians are very notorious for shooting their own people. They do not shoot them with a gun, but they draw a sword. They take the sword of slander, and slash and cut fellow-believers down.

It's often pride or self-righteousness, or a hurt feeling that causes believers to attack each other. Slander is a false weapon. Yes, we are to take up a sword - but which sword? Not the sword of slander, but the Sword of the Spirit of God. Never try to cut your brothers and sisters down. That is not your job, and you will be held accountable for taking it upon yourself to do so.

"Let all bitterness, wrath, anger, uproar, and slander be put away from you, along with all malice." (Ephesians 4:31)

Attend to casualties

What type of kingdom is it that leaves its wounded soldiers to die on the battle front? No nation will do that. To see its soldiers dying, unattended to; This will lead to a complete breakdown of the morale of the army. And we, as people of God and as soldiers, have to attend to our casualties in our battle against the enemy. If any fellow-believer has had a fall, let us go and lift him up. If he has been wounded, let's help him and nurse him or her to good health. Let us encourage one another to build the Kingdom of God.

More often than not, what a lot of people forget is that being a diplomat of another country and for that matter an ambassador of Christ is a specialised job which you just can't pick anyone from the street to occupy such an office. Therefore, the more of such people you lose, mean that to a lesser degree people with the expertise to play that role, and the less people with that expertise the slower government business would be accomplished. The Kingdom of Christ on earth has suffered and keeps on suffering because a lot of wounded soldiers have been left on the battle fields bleeding to death. A lot of ambassadors have been called back from duty and discarded whilst there are serious diplomatic issues requiring their expertise to be attended to.

Throughout the ancient, medieval and modern and the post-modern history of the church, the church has fought against itself, killed noblemen, sabotaged it future growth, introduced dogmas and tradition through certain acclaimed leaders which have come to haunt the church. Most of the time, the cause of this is ignorance of the true teachings of scripture and the over-emphasising of traditions. This leads to self-righteousness and its perpetuation in the church so long as it holds together. It seems as though the church's quest for self-righteousness other than the righteousness of God is in itself a besiegement of the enemy to deplete the church of vital resources in its battle against the enemy.

There are often certain self-seeking, greedy, self-righteous men and women of God that tend unknown to them, are used by the enemy as insiders to hurt the church. They become like Saul who due to religiosity thought he was doing the work of God by cleansing Israel of a sect that seems to threaten the fabric of the then Judeo-Roman world through their preaching of Christ. He murdered Christians and men of faith who would have had a more serious and a far-reaching impact with their ministry.

Unknown to him, he was acting upon an error although he was acting upon his knowledge of tradition and scripture, until he had an encounter with Christ. There are too many of us who know more of the tradition and regulations of the church than what the bible teaches and that's a scary thing to consider. People may act and find their actions to be satisfactory because it is correct as a tradition and the perspective on the church but not necessarily the perspective of God because it is simply not what the scriptures teach.

The church needs to rise and occupy her place as God's called out ones, the bride of Christ to influence the world positively.

"Brethren, if a man is caught in any trespass - in any sin - you who are spiritual, restore him in a spirit of gentleness. But watch yourself, lest you to be tempted." (Galatians 6:1)

This situation emphasizes the casualties within the church itself. If you have people in the church, who seem to be very religious and spiritual, but are self-righteously indifferent to brothers and sisters lying on the wayside, I would say, they are casualties. They are like the man Jesus told about - the one who was in the temple and prayed, *"God, I thank you that I am not like these other people."* (Luke 18:11)

Let us attend to our casualties! Let's encourage and build them up, that they might become strong and victorious in the Master.

Develop a right and a standard reaction to issues

"Walk in a manner worthy of the calling with which you have been called, with all humility and gentleness, with patience, showing forbearance to one another in love." (Ephesians 4:1-2)

There are circumstances you face every day that compels you to react in one way or another. Always seek, by the grace of the Lord, to make a right - a spiritual - reaction. If someone curses you, bless them. If they hit you on the cheek, let them hit the other cheek, also. If they steal from you, bless them.

Always seek to have the mind of Christ, in every reaction. It is so easy to fail in your reactions, both in the split-second reaction as well as the premeditated action. You may fail a hundred times in a day, but sometimes it's simply because you do not even realise that our reactions are part of the spiritual warfare.

Never take up any weapon that is not spiritual. Never resort to carnal weapons, weapons like retaliation or revenge – they are very wicked weapons! Somebody does something to me, so I return evil for evil. Oh how quickly that breaks down the walls of testimony.

"See that none render evil for evil unto any man; but ever follow that which is good, both among yourselves, and to all men."
(I Thessalonians 5:15)

Be fully armed

The Master has not left you defenceless. He gives you weapons and He shows you how to use them, and shows what His strategy is. Your legitimate weapons are spiritual weapons, and they all come from the King of Kings. The Master will never give you weapons that are not spiritual.

Breaking the Worry Habit: Live One Day at a Time

"Take therefore no thought for the morrow: for the morrow shall take thought for the things of itself. Sufficient unto the day is the evil thereof" (Matthew 6:34). One songwriter captured the words of our Lord in the following words of his song: *One day at a time, Lord Jesus, that's all I'm asking from you....*

The great secret of living a happy, healthy, holy and fruitful life is living without worry about the past and without anxiety regarding the future. The true child of God settles the past with God. Locking the past behind an iron door, he throws the key of remembrance away! The future is yet unborn, so he leaves that with God until it comes. Leaving the past and future with God, he summons all grace received, strength and courage to face the challenges of each day.

The following is how to break a worry habit in your life

Leave tomorrow with God and his good foresight

"Take therefore no thought for the morrow..." (Matthew 6:34)

It is an unnecessary distraction to worry or be anxious about tomorrow. There are men who waste their last hours on earth fretting over a morrow they never see! If we are preserved until the morrow, will it not bring with it tomorrow's good? What good can your worry do? It will not empty tomorrow of its problems and trials, but it empties today of its strength and comfort. Worrying about tomorrow will not enable you to escape future trouble; it only weakens you and makes you unfit to cope with those challenges when tomorrow eventually comes.

Worrying about tomorrow often leads to hurtful imagination, which produces wrong thinking and self-induced negative prophecies and tormenting fear. Do not try to cross the bridge before you get there, but cheerfully carry the cross of today and leave the future to God. He will be there before you get there. When tomorrow dawns, and its door swings open, the power and promises of God will be waiting for you to welcome you to a new day.

"As thy days, so shall thy strength be... " (Deuteronomy 33:25).

Labour today with God's guidance and great faith

We all pray for our daily bread. We can ask for strength to finish today's duty. Our business is with today; we can have divine supply for today's consumption. To import the possible burden of tomorrow into the duties of this day will decrease or deplete the strength which is meant for only today's responsibility. When tomorrow brings its burden, the God of tomorrow will bring with it sufficient grace and strength.

Today will require all the vigour we have to deal with its immediate "evils" or problems; there is no need to import cares from the future.

To load today with trials that have not really arrived would be to overload it. Anxiety is dangerous, but anxiety about things which have not yet happened is extremely dangerous, unnecessary venom that poisons and destroys us.

Worry about the future is useless; it achieves nothing. It is a pure waste of energy. Worrying about the future cripples you in the present; it lessens your efficiency with regard to today. The wisest thing is not to spend your energy looking for a solution to imaginary problems about the future which may never happen. Everyday has its problems and challenges; everyday has a daily quota of problems. If you want to go through life without being caged under unbearable loads of problems, treat each day as a unit. Do not carry yesterday or tomorrow with you. Live for today in God's strength and at the end of the day, rest in the Lord.

Let today be a gateway to a glorious future

Each day comes with problems and promises, obstacles and opportunities, burdens and benefits, disappointments and daily duties, setbacks and stepping stones. Welcome each day as a new gift from God. It comes with lessons to learn and challenges to face in order to strengthen your moral and spiritual muscles.

Welcome the day with a cheerful heart, saying, "This is the day!" (Psalm 118:24).

Yesterday is but a dream and tomorrow only a vision; but today well lived makes every yesterday a dream of happiness and every tomorrow a vision of hope. Today is your most precious possession, the only sure possession. It is unproductive to embitter the present by brooding and worrying over things that happened in the past. Worrying destroys our ability to think positively, and to concentrate on making positive changes. Receive each day as a gift from the Hands of your heavenly Father. Go through each day with the *"work of faith, and labour of love, and patience of hope in our Lord Jesus Christ"* (1 Thessalonians 1:3). Do something by the grace of God and through the strength supplied by the Holy Spirit each day. Let today and everyday be a gateway to a glorious future.

Take off the Limit

Many are not able to achieve success and greatness in all of life endeavours because of the several barriers before them. People talk about breakthroughs showing that there are forces and things limiting them, so they want the mighty power of God to break the limiting barriers before them. The truth is that most of the barriers are man-made. They are invisible walls that you get through negative thoughts that are built in your mind that limits and stops you from taking positive and powerful steps that will bring success and accomplishments. Negative thoughts build barriers that limit the thinker.

You cannot go higher than your thoughts will permit you. You cannot be greater than what you think and believe you can. Jesus taught that all things are possible to him that believes that it is possible.

"Jesus said unto him, if thou canst believe, all things are possible to him that believeth" (Mark 9:23)

These show that man is always limited by his thoughts.

- If a man does not believe a thing is possible, it means he can't do it or attain it.

- If you do not believe you will be healed, it doesn't matter who prays for you, you won't be healed.

- If you don't believe the money, you are looking for will come by God's intervention, it won't come.

- If you do not believe that the project, you are handling will be completed according to the original plan simply because there is a shortage of funds, it will be as you think.

- If you do not believe you can come out of lack and poverty, you will remain in that condition.

- If you do not believe you can be great though you came from a poor family, and no one in your family has ever made it to the top or attained greatness, you will remain small, insignificant, poor, and a non-achiever.

- If you do not believe you can forgive the one who has hurt you and move on with your life, you will continue to be tormented by the experience.

- If you do not believe you can overcome depression and enjoy your life, you will remain depressed all your life.

- If you do not believe that you will be promoted and continue to climb the ladder of success, you will remain at that spot.

The truth is that every man is limited by his thoughts and beliefs. That is why it is important that all have their minds renewed through the words of God and believe what it says and teaches.

Your thoughts limit the resources that will be made available to you.

Your thoughts limit the grace of God in your life. Your thoughts limit what the anointing of God can do in your life no matter who ministers to you by the name of the Lord Jesus Christ.

Your thoughts limit what God can do for you or with you.

God responds to our thoughts, and He judges us by what He finds us thinking.

Your thoughts prove faith or unbelief, and God responds only to faith.

If your thoughts are positive, God will definitely bless and keep His promises in your life.

"For as he thinketh in his heart, so is he: Eat and drink, saith he to thee; but his heart is not with thee." (Proverbs 23:7)

"But without faith it is impossible to please him:

for he that cometh to God must believe that he is, and that he is a rewarder of them that diligently seek him" (Hebrew 11:6)

BIBLIOGRAPHY

- Blank, W. (n.d.). *The Siege Of The City.* Retrieved from http://www.keyway.ca/htm2003/20030411.htm

- Ngabo, A. (n.d.). *Besiege (siege), tactics of war.* Retrieved from http://ngabo.org/prophetic/militarysystem/besiege_siege_tactics_of_war.html

- Burns, M. (n.d.). *Siege.* Retrieved from http://ft111.com/siege.htm

- Dew, D. (1997). *Spiritual Warfare.* Retrieved from http://dianedew.com/spirwar.htm

- Boyle, V. (2006). *The Power Of God In Christians To Overcome The Devil.* Retrieved from http://bible-truths-revealed.com/adv32.html

- Chelčický, P. (2009). *On The Spiritual Battle.* Retrieved from http://www.nonresistance.org/docs_pdf/On_The_Spiritual_Battle.pdf

- Angley, E. (1976). *The power of the Holy Ghost: The Anointing Breaks the Yoke* Retrieved from https://www.ernestangley.

- org/read/article/the_anointing_breaks_the_yoke

- Spiritual Warfare And Kingdom Strategy. (n.d.) Retrieved from http://www.maranathamrc.com/CONSTANT%20COMBAT%20PART%20FOUR.pdf

- Stephen. *(2009). Determination and Persistence.* Retrieved from http://academictips.org/blogs/determination-and-persistence/

- Onyemalech, S. (n.d.). *The siege is over.* Retrieved from http://www.jfoutreach.org/archives/archives/thesiegeisover.pdf

- Bostic, D. (n.d.). *Breaking the Cycle of Depression Part II.* Retrieved from http://www.truthandspiritministries.com/pdfs/depression3.pdf

- *Robbins, D. (1990).The Power of Praise & Worship.* Retrieved from http://www.victorious.org/praise.htm

- The Concise Oxford Dictionary. (12th ed.). (2011). Oxford, Oxford University Press.

www.ingramcontent.com/pod-product-compliance
Lightning Source LLC
Chambersburg PA
CBHW070937010826
48976CB00028B/2486